In so many ways, this was her dream come true. Could she really complain if it wasn't exactly perfect? "Yes. I will marry you, Konstantin."

"Good." He slid the cool ring onto her finger, then looped his arms behind her.

Eloise's hands were on his lapels, quivering with pleasure at having this right to touch him.

She looked up at him, expecting him to kiss her, but he only caressed the edge of her jaw with his bent finger.

He dipped his head into her throat and nuzzled his lips against her skin.

She gasped and shivered. Her nipples stung and her knees grew weak.

His breath pooled near her ear, fanning the arousal taking hold in her. This was surreal. Too perfect. Like a Christmas miracle. Not that she believed in such things, but maybe it was?

Canadian **Dani Collins** knew in high school that she wanted to write romance for a living. Twenty-five years later, after marrying her high school sweetheart, having two kids with him, working at several generic office jobs and submitting countless manuscripts, she got The Call. Her first Harlequin novel won the Reviewers' Choice Award for Best First in Series from *RT Book Reviews*. She now works in her own office, writing romance.

Books by Dani Collins

Harlequin Presents

Innocent in Her Enemy's Bed
Awakened on Her Royal Wedding Night
Marrying the Enemy

Four Weddings and a Baby

Cinderella's Secret Baby
Wedding Night with the Wrong Billionaire
A Convenient Ring to Claim Her
A Baby to Make Her His Bride

Bound by a Surrogate Baby

The Baby His Secretary Carries
The Secret of Their Billion-Dollar Baby

Diamonds of the Rich and Famous

Her Billion-Dollar Bump

Visit the Author Profile page
at Harlequin.com for more titles.

HUSBAND FOR THE HOLIDAYS

DANI COLLINS

Harlequin

PRESENTS

 Harlequin®
PRESENTS™

ISBN-13: 978-1-335-93927-2

Husband for the Holidays

Copyright © 2024 by Dani Collins

All rights reserved. No part of this book may be used or reproduced in any manner whatsoever without written permission.

Without limiting the author's and publisher's exclusive rights, any unauthorized use of this publication to train generative artificial intelligence (AI) technologies is expressly prohibited.

This is a work of fiction. Names, characters, places and incidents are either the product of the author's imagination or are used fictitiously. Any resemblance to actual persons, living or dead, businesses, companies, events or locales is entirely coincidental.

For questions and comments about the quality of this book, please contact us at CustomerService@Harlequin.com.

TM and ® are trademarks of Harlequin Enterprises ULC.

Harlequin Enterprises ULC
22 Adelaide St. West, 41st Floor
Toronto, Ontario M5H 4E3, Canada
www.Harlequin.com

Printed in Lithuania

MIX
Paper | Supporting responsible forestry
FSC® C021394

HUSBAND FOR THE HOLIDAYS

For Doug, my husband for holidays and all the rest of the days in the last thirty-plus years. Happy anniversary!

PROLOGUE

Seven years ago...

THE DOOR CLOSED behind her brother and Eloise Martin was left alone with the enigmatic Konstantin Galanis.

Her seventeen-year-old heart began to pound. Not with fear. Not exactly. Ilias was only running to the corner for eggnog and would be back in five minutes, but she was still overcome by something between awe and dread, as though she'd been left alone with a tiger and the promise that *he doesn't bite.*

Like heck. From what she'd read of his business acumen, Konstantin picked his teeth with the bones of his enemies every morning.

He was king of the jungle magnificent, too. He wore a stylish knitted pullover in ivory with brown suede patches on the elbows and the tops of his shoulders. His jeans were black, matching his short boots. His hair was cut short around his ears and was rakishly windswept on top. Given it was late afternoon, a hint of shadow was coming in on his jaw, framing his somber mouth and accentuating the hollows in his cheeks. His brows were strong thick lines over eyes that were cast down to ignore her in favor of his phone.

This crush of hers was silly. Childish. She knew it was,

but she'd never been able to shake it. While her friends swooned over a cute actor or a boy band star, she secretly took screenshots of Konstantin from news releases and imagined a world where she was part of his life.

It was so immature! Especially when she was looking at him now and all she felt was intimidated and mesmerized.

He must have sensed her staring. His spiky lashes lifted and his dark brown gaze snared hers. Her pupils dilated in reaction. The lights on the tree suddenly seemed to paint the whole room in psychedelic reds and blues and golds and greens.

Quit gawking, she ordered herself and shakily turned back to the tree she was supposed to be decorating.

She didn't allow herself to look over her shoulder. He'd probably gone back to reading his phone, but her acute awareness of him had her imagining she felt his gaze traveling down her back and bottom and legs. She grew clumsy as she took each ornament from its case and looped it onto a branch.

"Ilias said you came to New York to settle some business with him." Nerves made her voice off-key and sharp.

Silence, except for the music switching to "Santa Baby."

She looked over at him.

He *was* looking at her, which made her pulse hitch.

"Yes," he replied.

"I don't…" She cleared her throat, feeling extra awkward. "I know that Galanis is a freight and shipping enterprise, but I don't know what you do there." She had the impression it was more involved than managing an inherited fortune the way her brother did.

"I oversee it. We're expanding into media and tech so it's being rebranded as KGE."

"You run it by yourself?" She hung the next ornament and glanced over.

"I have employees."

He made her feel gauche, quirking his mouth in that ironic way.

"I meant that it sounds like a lot to shoulder for one person." He was twenty-five, same as Ilias, even though he projected an air that was light-years ahead of everyone on the planet in maturity and life experience. "I only wondered if you have brothers or sisters who help?" Ilias had never mentioned any siblings and gossip sites were distressingly vague when it came to Konstantin's personal life.

"No," Konstantin replied.

"Other family?" His grandfather had died a few years ago.

"No."

This was going well. "Pets?" she asked facetiously.

"No," he pronounced dryly. "What do you really want to know? How I came to live with my grandfather? I don't talk about it."

Well, that was clear enough, wasn't it?

"I wasn't trying to be nosy." She ignored the sting of his less than subtle rebuff and hung another ornament, this one shaped like an icicle. The heat in her cheeks should have caused it to melt into a puddle on the floor. "You and Ilias have been friends forever." Since their boarding school days in England. "But he's never told me much about you."

Ilias had rarely brought his friend around. Aside from early glimpses over the tablet, Eloise had only seen Konstantin in person a handful of times. This was the first time in well over five years that she'd spoken to him in person, but she'd been idolizing him from the first time she heard his voice.

"Good."

"What? I mean, pardon?" She had forgotten what they were talking about.

"I'm glad he doesn't gossip about me. I'm a private person."

Okay, then.

She stifled a sigh and looked toward the door. Was Ilias milking the cow and growing the nutmeg himself? What was taking him so long?

She moved to the dining table and started to carry one of the chairs toward the tree.

"What are you doing?" Konstantin was beside her in three long strides, sending a jolt of electricity through her blood.

"I'm a shortcake." She was pointing out the obvious. It was the bane of her existence that she was barely five feet tall, especially at times like this when she found herself staring into the middle of a man's chest, feeling at every disadvantage because of her size. "I can't reach the top branches."

"I'll do it. Show me what you want." He replaced the chair, body almost brushing hers, fritzing her brain cells.

He moved to the tree and waited with bored expectation.

"I'm not one of those people with a rigid set of rules around how the tree looks." She made herself move closer even though she was walking right up to the tiger with his razor-sharp claws and giant teeth. "I just pick something from the box and stick it in a bare spot."

It wasn't rocket science, but he took the frosted globe from her hand, held it near a top branch, then looked at her again.

"Sure." She shrugged.

A snowflake went next, then a snowman. Each time,

he checked with her before he looped the string around the branch.

"Have you never decorated a tree before?" she asked with bemusement.

"No."

"I guess that shouldn't surprise me. Mom hasn't hung her own decorations in years. If I hadn't come to spend the holidays with Ilias, he probably wouldn't bother, either. I like doing it, though. Put this one here." She extended the reindeer as high as she could.

His fingers brushed hers as he took it.

They were standing really close. Close enough that she caught the faded scent of his aftershave and the traces of the rum he'd taken straight because they'd run out of eggnog.

The music switched to Mariah Carey crooning "All I Want for Christmas Is You."

As Eloise looked up at him, Konstantin looked down at her and their gazes tangled. The world tilted and Eloise fell into an abyss.

Oh. Something happened within her. She had always felt giddy and nervous around him. Awestruck. She thought he was beautiful and compelling and she had always longed for him to like her. To *notice* her.

She hadn't realized it would be like this, though. She was old enough that she garnered sexual attention. Sometimes it was flattering, other times unwelcome.

It had never felt reciprocal. Not until now. The sensation was like an implosion that compressed heat into her, then expanded in an all-over blush of pleasure.

Konstantin looked at her the way a man looked at a woman and whatever cocoon she'd been occupying was suddenly too confining. She wanted to break out and step out and open herself. She felt fragile as a butterfly, but weighted, too. As though her blood were made of molasses.

That's what his eyes were made of, she thought distantly: dark gold bittersweet molasses. And his mouth...

Her heart fluttered as she willed him to kiss her.

The keypad beeped and the lock hummed. Ilias called out, "They didn't have the good kind. We'll have to make do."

Konstantin moved to the table where he'd left his phone and pocketed it, then met Ilias in the foyer.

"I have to get back to Athens."

"What? Why?"

Ilias's shock echoed hers. She moved closer to eavesdrop, hearing the rustle of Konstantin's overcoat as he slipped it on. His voice lowered, but she heard his rumbled words.

"Your sister is cute, but I don't want to encourage her."

Oh, Gawd.

She covered her face, mortified that she'd misinterpreted that moment and made such a fool of herself that Konstantin couldn't even stick around to face her.

"I'd hoped she'd grown out of that." Ilias's voice held humor. "Thanks for not making me call you out for pistols at dawn. We'll talk soon."

The door closed and she wanted to run into her room and hide. She made herself go back to the tree and pretend she hadn't overheard anything.

"That looks good," Ilias said behind her. At least he was kind enough not to tease her.

"I think so," she lied, refusing to look at him. She hated this tree. The whole season was ruined. Based on how sick she felt, she doubted she would ever enjoy Christmas again.

CHAPTER ONE

Present day...

THE TWELVE DAYS of Christmas was turning into twelve nights of acute anxiety.

Eloise glanced again to be sure she had the right name on the present and knocked on the door of the Manhattan high-rise apartment.

A woman in silk slacks and a cowl-neck sweater answered the door. Her blond hair was in a ponytail, but the loose, messy kind that had been teased to look casual. Her makeup was fresh enough to signal she had plans for the evening. She gave Eloise's elf costume a pithy once-over and sighed.

Eloise knew what an atrocity it was. Even the smallest uniform had been too big for her and the fabric was so cheap static made it cling in all the wrong places. Plaits of orange yarn protruded from either side of her green bent cone hat behind pointed ears. The whole thing was probably askew because the yarn was itchy and she kept flicking it away from her face. Fake fur trimmed the green vest she wore over a long-sleeved turtleneck of red-and-white stripes. Her green skirt fell to mid-thigh and ended in triangles adorned with bells. Her legs were made to look like candy canes complete with shoes that turned up at the toes.

She was a caricature looking at a version of the affluent person she used to be.

"Good evening," she said with a polite smile. "I believe the doorman announced me? You ordered Twelve Days for Noah?"

"My sister-in-law did. She must be mad at me." The woman turned to call out, "Noah? There's someone here to see you."

"Again?" A four-year-old boy ran to the door in his pajamas.

"Hi, Noah!" Eloise crouched and dug deep for a voice that was playful and filled with the magic and wonder of the season. "I'm Merrilee. I think you met Rocket yesterday? I'm another one of Santa's helpers. He asked me to bring you this." She offered the gift.

"*Cool*!" He grabbed the gift. "Can I open it?" He was already retreating back into the apartment.

"Say thank you first," the woman said in a harried voice.

"Thank you," Noah called back, but he was gone.

"See you tomorrow," Eloise said as she stood, but the door was already shutting in her face. "Merry Christmas," she added, faint and facetious.

She might once have been as rich and well-dressed as that woman, but she had never been that awful to people who were just trying to make ends meet. She had definitely taken for granted living in places like this, though. And having plans on Tuesday night and being showered with gifts just because.

She dragged her oversized velvet sack full of gifts back to the elevator. It was affixed to a square of wood on casters and was worse than walking a dog, wandering every direction and clipping her heel when she least expected it.

Once in the elevator, she dug for the next parcel, checking the time and the address on her phone. The building was only a few blocks away, but dragging this cloth bag through the streets was a lot harder than it looked. Snow clogged up the casters and—

Wait. Were there two kids at this next address? She pawed deeper into the bag, vaguely aware the elevator had halted and the doors opened to the lobby. This one? She turned the gift over inside the bag.

"Up or out?" a gruff male voice asked with tested patience.

That voice.

She jerked her attention upward and recognition crashed over her along with a hormonal rush of yearning that nearly took out her knees.

Oh, my God.

Horror followed because she did not want Konstantin Galanis to see her like this.

He wasn't even looking at her. His profile was every bit as remote and compelling as she remembered, every bit as dismissive as he stood to the side, holding the open door to give her room to exit while he looked toward the front doors of the building.

He was as impossibly good-looking as she remembered, too, broodingly handsome with his black hair and stern brow and strong freshly shaved jaw. His overcoat hung open over a cranberry-colored jacket, a pleated shirt and tuxedo trousers.

Did he live in this building? Or—

He started to turn his head, probably wondering what was taking her so long. She ducked her head in panic, wanting to dive into this giant sack of hers and disappear. Hunching her chin into her chest, she scurried past him, sack veering uncontrollably behind her.

"Hey. How'd that go?" the overly friendly doorman asked her as he brought her coat and boots from his parcel shelf behind his desk.

"Fine." Horrible. Worst night ever and she had some doozies to compare to.

"Are you coming back tomorrow?" He was mid-twenties, same as her. His smile invited her to linger and chat, but she didn't have time. Or inclination.

"Depends on the schedule. I'm a spare, covering for whoever calls in, but it's only Day Four. I'm sure I'll be back here at some point." As she spoke, she hurried to toe off her silly shoes and zipped into her knee-high boots, then shrugged on her coat, still feeling as though Konstantin were standing over there staring at her when he had definitely already forgotten about her and was twenty stories up by now.

"Let me give you my number. Maybe we can have a drink—" The doorman's expression changed into one that was more professional. "I'm sorry, sir. Is there a problem with the elevator?"

Eloise glanced up from tucking her curly shoes into the sack, realizing that Konstantin was still here in the lobby, still holding the doors open while he stared at her with a thunderstruck look on his face.

No! Her stomach curdled. She ducked her head again, skipped the switch of hat and finding her gloves. She didn't even belt her coat before she yanked the sack toward the door, desperate to get away before—

"Eloise!"

No, no, no.

She pushed out the door, cringing more from hearing her name behind her than the slap in the face of a blustery winter evening in New York.

She kept walking, letting the door drop closed behind her. It was rude. So rude. But it had been bad enough that he'd seen her like this and *hadn't* recognized her. Why should he? It had been six years since her brother's funeral. Before that, it had been that awful Christmas when she had imprinted on him like a duckling on a drake.

"Eloise." He was right behind her, commanding her to stop.

"I'm on a tight schedule," she said, refusing to look at him. "Children are waiting."

It was true. The sort of indulgent parent who booked twelve days of personal deliveries for their children were not the type to be inconvenienced. If they said the delivery should happen before little Sally went to bed at seven o'clock, then that was the time the knock should resound on the door.

And who had designed these stupid sacks? Satan? She felt as though she were pulling a fully loaded sled.

"You can spare me five minutes." Konstantin caught her arm.

Even through the layers of her coat and shirt, she felt the sizzle. She had managed to convince herself that weird moment seven years ago had been the product of a desperate, juvenile imagination. That she was over her crush and didn't expect any man to save her, least of all this one.

But, ugh. She immediately felt the pull. The draw.

She shook it and him off.

"I really can't." She pressed on to the end of the block, then had to stop to wait for the walk signal.

She couldn't resist glancing up to see that he'd stayed

right beside her, though. Damn him for keeping up with his long legs and no effort. He looked perfect, of course, with snowflakes landing on his dark hair and the collar of his overcoat turned up like a secret agent from the cold war. His eyes were still that depthless dark brown, not that she could tell in the flash of headlights and the liminal glow off the snow. She only remembered the color because she had been so fascinated by his eyes those other times. She wished she understood how his bottomless, steady gaze could cause such a trembling sensation inside her. When he looked straight at her this way, she felt as though he were pulling her soul from the depths of her body.

People began crossing the street. She lurched to go with them, to escape.

He caught the edge of her sack, preventing it from leaving the curb.

"I don't want to get fired." She turned back and tried to yank the edge from his grip, but he closed his fist tighter.

"Why are you working at all? At *this*?" His disparaging tone told her exactly what he thought of her job, but it was honest work. It was better than the forced marriage her stepfather had tried to sell her into.

That was the real humiliation. That her life had descended to this. Not just working to support herself. There was no shame in that. It was the part where she had failed to protect her mother and they were both victims of a con artist. It was the fact that she had allowed herself to live like a spoiled princess, never questioning where the money came from, so she'd been completely unequipped when the vault was slammed closed against her.

It was the fact that the one man her brother had looked up to was looking down on her.

Frustrated by all of that, she stepped around the sack

so she was right beside him. She grabbed the velvet near where he held it and yanked it free of his grip, then turned to lurch across the street. But now the sack was in front of her, causing her to trip forward onto it.

In the same millisecond, the light changed. A car accelerated to take the corner before the oncoming traffic crossed the intersection.

There was a honk and a flash of a headlight, a shout and a sensation of being snatched out of the air like a sparrow into the claws of a hawk. There was a horrible crunching noise that made her cringe into the wall of wool as she waited for whatever injury she'd sustained to explode with pain.

"Look before you cross the street!" Konstantin's harsh voice blasted against her ear. His arms were banded around her, squeezing the breath out of her. One hand was splayed on the back of her head, tucking her face into his overcoat.

She hadn't been hit. She had fistfuls of his sleeves in her hands while her feet pedaled to find the sidewalk. Her heart was rattled and thumping, her ears ringing. The fragrance of aftershave filled her nostrils, going straight into her brain like a drug.

A wave of helplessness tried to engulf her, one that urged her to melt into his tempered strength and cry. She was cold and tired and hungry and scared. And there was also that older, ingrained and immature longing for exactly this: to be rescued and coddled and held by him.

She refused to buckle to any of that.

"Let me go," she muttered, struggling even as he loosened his hold and let her slide to the ground.

He had to steady her as her foot slid in the slush, then she was free of his touch and felt utterly bereft.

"I have to—oh, no!" The sack had spilled off the curb.

Two gifts were half crushed by tire tracks while the limp velvet sat in an icy puddle, collecting a dusting of wet snow. "What am I supposed to do now?"

"That could have been you. Do you realize that?" He sounded livid, which stung because she had only ever wanted his approval.

She started to bend, wanting to see if there was anything to be salvaged.

"You're not crawling in the gutter after useless parcels." He caught her back, his clasp on her arm keeping her standing beside him. "The sanitation people will clean it up when they do their rounds."

"I have to deliver these toys. I'll lose my job if I don't." She waved her free hand at the disaster.

"What sort of foolish job is it?"

"It's called Twelve Days of Christmas. Parents sign up for twelve days of personal deliveries for their children. They're *expecting* me." She shook off his hold.

"They'll survive. You may not," he added scathingly. "Come." He tried to turn her back the way they'd come.

She dug her boots into the clumping snow. "I need my job if I want to eat." That had been a harsh lesson, but she'd sure learned it in the last eight months.

"I'll feed you." He looped his arm behind her in an arched cage that swept her along like a blade plowing snow. "While you eat, you can tell me what the hell has happened that you're resorting to this."

Her feet stumbled to keep up with him while her back absorbed his strength all the way into her blood cells.

"You're acting like I'm dealing drugs." She looked back at the carnage of her paycheck, losing any chance at keeping her job when a figure darted out of the shadows to claim the sack and what was left of the parcels. They dragged all of it around the corner.

She couldn't begrudge someone living on the street for seizing an opportunity. She had a better understanding of poverty these days. She was even a little glad that some poor soul would enjoy something like a Secret Santa windfall, but it only reinforced that she was *very* fired.

Konstantin cursed under his breath and dropped his arm from around her as they arrived under the awning of the building they'd just left.

A beautiful woman had just walked out and—

Wait. Was that Gemma Wilkinson, the actress? She was red carpet–ready in a pine green gown under a black wrap. Her hair was up, her ears adorned with diamonds and her smoky eyes were trained on them with appalled astonishment.

"I asked Giles what was keeping you and he said you walked out. I thought you were having a cigarette."

"Something has come up." Konstantin didn't introduce Eloise or even look at her, only told Gemma, "I can't take you to the party tonight."

Gemma's incredulous laughter was aimed directly at Eloise in her crooked ears and ugly hat.

Where were catastrophic events when you needed them? Or even just a clear path of escape? A dog walker was behind her, the mesh of leashes hemming her into this curbside carnival act.

"Konstantin," Gemma said in a purr of sensual warning. "If you don't take me to that party tonight, you won't take me anywhere. Ever."

"Fair." It was one of the most dispassionate responses Eloise had ever witnessed and she'd seen the complete lack of pity in the eyes of the landlord when he'd informed her and her roommate that rent would double on January first.

Konstantin withdrew his phone and brought it to his ear, saying to Gemma, "I need my car right now, but I can send it back for you if you like."

"Oh, don't bother," Gemma said with subdued fury and spun to reenter the building.

The dog walker and the doorman and two passersby were all witnessing this drama. Eloise wanted to die. She truly did.

While Konstantin was on the phone, however, she seized the chance to call her supervisor—who was not paid nearly enough to care about the details of what had happened.

"So you'll miss the last five deliveries?" she summed up briskly. "I'll contact the customers and reschedule. You know I can't use you again?"

"I know. I'll turn in my uniform tomorrow. Oh. Except I lost the shoes."

"I'll tell head office you were hit by the car. That way they won't take the cost of the gifts out of your pay."

Wow. The Christmas spirit was alive and well. "Thanks. Merry Christmas."

"You, too, hon."

As she pocketed her phone, a gleaming SUV pulled up to the curb. Konstantin stepped forward to open the back door himself, waving her to climb inside.

"I think you've mistaken me for your date. I'll head to the subway—"

"Get in."

She curled her cold hands into fists, suspecting her gloves were in the lost sack since they weren't in her pockets.

"You want to know what happened to make me take a

job like this? I refused to buckle to an overbearing man."
Take that, she added with a lift of her chin that made the
bell on her hat give a muted tinkle.

"How's that working out for you?"

Not great, obviously. That didn't mean she should buckle
to him.

"Get in, Eloise. Or I'll put you in."

She held his I-mean-it stare and to her eternal shame,
frissons of excitement curled through her abdomen. She
wanted his hands on her. The sparks of attraction she'd
always harbored for him continued to smolder inside her.

"Do I have to count to three?" His patronizing tone
called her a child. It was the ultimate insult, considering
the very adult things she'd had to deal with lately.

Somehow, she channeled the privileged socialite her
mother had taught her to be.

"Since it's your fault I lost my job, you may buy me dinner." She held his gaze as she passed under his nose, then
clambered into the vehicle with a musical rattle of the bells
on her skirt.

CHAPTER TWO

KONSTANTIN WALKED AROUND to the door that his driver opened for him, taking these few seconds to shake off the last of the adrenaline that had punched through him when Eloise had almost stepped into traffic. That had been the most terrifying—

No. He never let emotions of any variety sweep over him. When things didn't go as planned, he took control of himself and the situation, made adjustments and carried on.

This was quite the unexpected detour, though. Not that he'd wanted to attend tonight's soiree. Gemma had insisted. Since he had invited her to accompany him to the Maldives, Konstantin had relented, but the party wasn't even raising money for a good cause. It was purely a see-and-be-seen thing, something he loathed and typically avoided.

He settled into the captain's chair behind the driver and looked across the console to Eloise in the other one, studying her as the glow on the overhead bulb faded and his driver pulled into traffic. Between the painted freckles and round pink circles adorning her cheeks, and the hat and yarn that hid her real hair, he had almost missed recognizing her.

His only thought while he'd waited for the elevator had been that he couldn't wait to leave New York. He could stand the bustle and honks, but the relentless assault of seasonal cheer, of carols and blinking lights and jangling bells, almost made him nostalgic for the deprivations of his childhood. Winters back then had been damp and gray. He'd shivered so hard his teeth had hurt and the only escape had been the rocky slopes and barren vineyards of northeastern Greece, but at least it had been quiet.

When the elevator opened and yet another ludicrous manifestation of the season appeared before him—a young woman in an elf costume—he'd barely looked at her. He'd had the sense she was staring at him, but that was normal. Konstantin owned a conglomerate worth billions. He didn't seek the spotlight, but he often earned reactions of awe and deference.

While his front brain essentially ignored her the way he ignored any staff who were getting on with their work, some preternatural sense had prickled to life in him as she brushed past. Once she was out, he should have stepped into the empty elevator to get on with his life, but his inner beast had snatched a look at a retreating woman, gauging her to be *not* a teenager as he'd first assumed.

She was petite, yes, and her clothing was an eyesore, but the doorman was hitting on her, indicating she was old enough to drink.

Konstantin had been irritated by that other man's attention toward her, which had been irritating in itself. What the hell did he care? He wasn't the possessive type even when he was in a relationship. This stranger was nothing to him. She wasn't even the kind of woman who usually caught his eye. He preferred tall curvy blondes who looked him in the eye and radiated sexual confidence. He slept with women who knew their own worth and went after what they wanted, even if it was him and his fortune. At least he knew where he stood and that they were capable of looking after themselves.

Vulnerable waifs were a hard no.

But he'd lingered to watch the interplay and listen to her speak. Even as the neutral elocution that denoted a cultured education was hitting his ears and ringing bells, she shook out her coat.

It wasn't a remarkable coat. Konstantin had seen many like it on various women through the years. It was a classic trench-style lined with a signature plaid from a popular designer. It looked well-worn so maybe she'd picked it up from a thrift store because it seemed high-end for someone in her position.

Yet, it fit her perfectly.

And suddenly Konstantin had heard a voice from the grave.

I have to buy my sister a coat. Something warm. She's coming for Christmas and I don't want her to be cold.

The ground had shifted beneath him. A flare of something dangerous had whooshed alight inside him. It was a reaction he had deliberately distanced himself from the first time he'd felt it. And the second.

But as she flashed him a last persecuted glance, he finally *saw* her. It was a gut punch and a knee to the groin and an awakening of something primal in him that he didn't even know he possessed.

She ignored his call of her name, which propelled him outside after her. None of this made sense. What the *hell* was Ilias's little sister doing, trudging through a snowstorm in a Peter Pan costume, dragging a sack like she was moving a dead body in a cheap detective movie?

She was aggressively ignoring him. Still. As the vehicle

moved forward in the heavy traffic, she kept her stiff profile turned to the busy sidewalk beyond her side window.

"I told you to contact me if you needed anything," he reminded her. "Why haven't you?"

She made a noise between a choke and a laugh. "That was six years ago. At a funeral. You were being polite."

To some extent, perhaps, but... "I always mean what I say."

No response.

"How is Lilja?" he asked of her mother.

"Fine."

"In the same way that you're fine?"

She drew a deep breath, as though ready to launch into a lengthy reply, then said a cryptic, "She remarried a few years ago." Her breath hissed out and her chin went down. Her fingers twined together in her lap. "They live in Nice."

"I heard about that." Distantly. He had had his assistant send an appropriate gift expressing his felicitations. "Are *you* married?" It was a jarring thought that had him recollecting her remark about not buckling to an overbearing man.

"No," she said pithily.

"Living with someone?" Who was looking after her? Because it wasn't herself.

"I have a roommate," she said, talking to the window again.

"Are you using drugs?"

"*No*," she cried. "Why would you think—" She clammed up.

Exactly. Given her upbringing, finding her like this defied logic.

They arrived outside Konstantin's building. Eloise leaned to peer upward.

"Is there a restaurant up there somewhere?"

"I'm not sitting in a restaurant with Santa's Little Helper."

"You're not kidnapping one, either. That sort of behavior puts you on the Naughty list."

"I've never been on the Nice one," he drawled as he stepped out into the gust of wind and peck of snow. He liked to believe he was civilized and fair, but nice? No. That skated too close to caring and sentiment. He wasn't one to be *moved*.

Eloise had left the SUV and was standing on the sidewalk under the awning when he got there, hugging her coat lapels tight under her throat.

"I'd rather go home. Which way is the subway?" She squinted into the wall of flakes falling on either side of the awning.

"You said I could buy you dinner. Oscar will pick up our meal." He nodded at his driver to leave and the car pulled away. "Come wash your face and tell me what's going on."

He started toward the entrance, but she stayed where she was.

"Really?" He stepped back to face her. "We've been alone before. Nothing happened." It was a lie. Something had happened to him the last two times he'd seen her, but he'd put the brakes on before he stepped over any lines.

At least, he believed that until her gaze flashed up. Her hazel eyes reflected the white lights roped around the potted trees that lined the carpet to the door. He caught a glimpse of something in her eyes that was so naked, he felt the jolt of it travel into his chest and zing into his gut and groin.

Her lashes swept down, breaking that connection, but the electrical lines inside him were still smoking and tingling.

That was what he had turned away from twice before.

She sparked a sexual reaction in him that was not only inappropriate, it was as dangerous as a keg of dynamite. He had walked away those other times because she'd been too young. She'd been grieving. And she was his best friend's kid sister.

He could have done it again right now. She wanted to leave and he could let her. He wasn't stupid enough to bring explosives into his home and start playing with matches.

But he couldn't let her go, either. She wasn't even wearing gloves or a proper hat.

"If I wanted sex tonight, I would have gone on my date," he said tersely, hoping to alleviate that worry from her mind. "This outfit of yours is not as seductive as you think it is."

"Rude." She scowled at him, but she was shivering.

Ilias's voice was in his ear again. *I don't want her to be cold.*

"Come inside," Konstantin insisted. "Your brother would expect me to help you."

"That's emotional manipulation," Eloise accused with affront.

"It's the truth." He glowered at her.

Eloise rolled her lips together. A strange hotness had arrived behind her eyes and in the back of her throat. She missed Ilias *all the time*. The promise of talking to someone who remembered him, who had cared about him even a fraction as much as she had, was tempting enough to override all her reservations.

She wasn't really afraid of Konstantin, anyway. She was afraid of her outsized reaction to him. The tiniest little remark seemed to slide straight through her skin and leave a wide bruise.

But she was freezing and hungry and her brother would have at least expected her to give his best friend a few minutes of her time.

Also, *she* wanted to give Konstantin her time.

She sighed and walked to the door into the building, allowing him to reach past her and open it for her.

This high-rise was even nicer than the ones she'd been delivering gifts to. The elevator he guided her into read Private above the doors. Konstantin's fingerprint triggered the single button inside it and it shot skyward in silence.

Eloise wasn't a stranger to wealth. She'd grown up benefiting from the Drakos fortune, the one her mother had married into and her brother had inherited. She had attended a top boarding school and skied St. Moritz and shopped Paris and Milan every season.

Konstantin was way above that, though. Maybe if he had survived, Ilias would have kept up with Konstantin, but maybe not. Ilias had commented once that Konstantin was *driven in a way I never will be*. She had always wondered if that had anything to do with Konstantin being an orphan, but who knew with him. He was a private person, as he'd made clear more than once.

The doors opened into a two-story mansion that took up the entire top of the building.

"Let me take your coat."

She hadn't had anyone stand behind her and act so chivalrous in a long time. It gave her a shiver as his fingertips grazed her shoulders. She slipped off her boots and felt drawn to peer into his home.

A floating staircase rose on one side. The main floor was an open living space within an arced wall of windows that offered views of the Hudson River and New York Harbor.

Comfortable furniture beckoned under gentle lighting and a central fireplace clicked on as she approached it.

"You don't have a tree," she noted.

"I'm leaving tomorrow." Konstantin had removed his overcoat, revealing his red jacket, crisp white shirt, bow tie and black trousers.

She swallowed, freshly accosted by his good looks, but also reminded that he'd been going on a date. A clench of envy squeezed her heart, one that had barbs of inadequacy attached to it. Her whole life, she'd wished to be taller and curvier and capable of exuding authority. Instead, she was "cute"—she loathed that descriptor—and funny and rarely taken seriously. She folded her arms, chilled despite the warmth coming off the flickering flames next to her.

"I can't take you seriously in that." He started up the stairs. "Come."

She cautiously followed him and halted at the double doors to his bedroom. It was expansive and luxurious, with a huge four-poster bed and a sitting area with a desk.

He sent her a pithy look as he peeled off his jacket. "You're my friend's baby sister. My designs on you are strictly platonic."

He disappeared into a walk-in closet, coming back with a pair of drawstring track pants, a blue T-shirt, a cable knit pullover and a fresh pair of white socks.

"Change in there. Help yourself to whatever you need." He nodded at where a pair of doors stood open, revealing a bathroom twice the size of the apartment she currently shared with a roommate and her roommate's on-again, off-again girlfriend.

Eloise gathered the clothes and inched into the show-piece of marble and gleaming gold taps. She took in the freestanding tub before the bank of windows, the massive sauna shower and—

"Why is the toilet behind a clear wall?" she called. "Is this a break glass in case of emergency situation or…?"

He walked in and touched a button that cast the cubicle in a gentle glow while darkening its clear walls to opaque.

"Oh. Fancy." She couldn't help glancing longingly at the tub. Her building hadn't had proper hot water in weeks. She'd been making do with birdbaths and heavy use of deodorant.

"Do you want a bath?" He pulled his shirt from his trousers.

Her whole body flushed in panicked confusion. He had *just* said—

"Alone," he said dryly, popping his cuffs.

She was starting to despise that patronizing look of his.

"Come downstairs whenever you're ready." He walked out, pulling the bathroom doors closed behind him.

CHAPTER THREE

ELOISE LATCHED THE DOORS, planning to change quickly, get through dinner, then get herself home where she could start searching for a job to replace the one she'd lost.

Temptation got the better of her. Maybe it was vanity. Or cowardice.

Facing Konstantin was becoming more daunting by the second, especially when she looked as bedraggled as she felt. She hated that he was seeing her at her very worst.

Not that she'd looked great at the funeral. No wonder he had pushed her away *again* that day.

She swept that awful memory from her mind and hurried to wash her face.

Somewhere between drying her face and getting undressed, however, she found herself starting the shower. She wanted a few minutes to pull herself together, and yes, wanted to feel the way she used to feel when her needs were abundantly met and her problems were mostly superficial.

Seconds later, she was under the soft rain of the warm water, almost moaning aloud. *This shampoo.* The lather was silky, the conditioner rich as melted butter. The body wash smelled of sage and agave and made her skin tingle with rejuvenation.

She could have stayed here all night, but made herself

step out and bit back another groan when she realized the towels were heated. The robe she stole off the hook was luxuriously soft and smelled like the body wash, as though Konstantin had worn it against his own clean, naked skin earlier today.

Oh, why was she like this? She'd had years to find a man who interested her as much as Konstantin, but he had set an impossible bar. She kept looking for someone with his same balance of intellect, confidence, sophistication and wit coupled with raw, masculine sex appeal.

Me and every other woman on the planet, she thought dourly.

Konstantin didn't even see her as a woman, only as his friend's *baby* sister.

We've been alone before. Nothing happened.

She closed her eyes, trying to block out the memory of finding him in the garden of her mother's villa in Athens. The rest of the guests had gone home. She'd been tired, so tired, but the service was over, the house was empty and her mother had gone to bed.

"Thank you for everything you've done," she had said, hovering on the final step of the stairs to the lower terrace. "It means a lot."

Silently, she had begged him to open up in some way, to reveal he was as gutted as she was or hold her maybe, so she didn't have to be the strong one.

He turned and came toward her, but stopped in front of her without touching her.

"You'll call me if you need anything." His voice was raspy, but that was the sum total of emotion he revealed.

She didn't doubt that he was affected, though. He had to be. He had been in America when Ilias's small plane had gone down. He'd offered to identify him and had then made all the arrangements for Ilias to come back to Athens.

"I will," she agreed and hugged herself.

"You shouldn't be out here without a coat." He touched her arm. It was only protected by the sheer black sleeve of her dress.

"I don't feel it," she said in a dull voice. "I'm so numb I can't even cry."

"Don't cry," he commanded gruffly and stepped closer, enfolding her.

She was still on the step so the top of her head was right under his chin. She leaned into him and the sweetness of being held by this man, whom she had been alternately yearning for and cursing since last Christmas, began to break through her shell.

He was warm and strong and seemed to care, really care.

Without any conscious thought to it, she let her folded arm slide upward to curl around his neck. She stood on her tiptoes on that step and turned her face into his neck, tilting her mouth up to brush his jaw.

There was a sharp inhale as he stiffened. He looked down at her and their mouths brushed. His hands hardened on her and his mouth opened across hers in a rough claim that dragged her from a yearning for comfort into a cyclone of twisted emotions: anger and sorrow, pain and assuagement. A spike of pure, carnal hunger that jolted like lightning into her belly.

Then he wrenched his head up with a curse and pressed her away from him.

"That's not—get inside. I'll see myself out." He had left her there, swaying and stunned.

The tears had finally come. She had collapsed on the concrete stairs and cried so hard she couldn't walk or speak.

It had been pure hell, leaving her with a bruised heart and a terrible cold, but at least she'd been able to resent him and blame him after that. Her crush had been crushed. She hadn't seen him again until today.

But he insisted nothing had happened.

She cringed, hating that he still had this effect on her! And how was he supposed to see her as a grown-up if she was dressed in his giant-ass clothes? She held the track pants against herself, thinking they'd look as ludicrous as the elf costume.

She left the humid bathroom and brought the clothes back to the bedroom, planning to enter his walk-in closet to find something else, but she lost her nerve.

At least the robe was more of a one-size-fits-all. It probably only fell to his shins while hitting the floor on her. Same for the cuffs. They fell past her wrists, but the thick velour was warm and snuggly and very comforting.

She dropped his clothes on the foot of the bed and belted the robe tighter. Then she found a comb and worked on her hair. She hadn't had it cut in ages so the tangles fell past her shoulders, taking forever to work out.

Konstantin had left the bedside lamp burning. Otherwise, the room was quiet and dark, allowing her to move to the window where she admired the sparkle of city lights and the few boats moving across the iced waterways.

She sank onto the sofa, letting her arms take a rest in her lap, thinking…

She was too tired to think. Too tired to talk. What would she even say? Everything had become very difficult and grim. Unbearable.

She blocked it out by closing her eyes. She resented that he wanted her to face him and find the words to defend her choices. To explain…

She sighed. At least when she was running flat out, trying to stay afloat, she didn't have to dwell. She didn't have to feel. She didn't have to…

She yawned and let herself tip onto her side. She pulled a cushion under her cheek, needing to rest just for a minute…

Eloise hadn't come down by the time dinner arrived so Konstantin went back upstairs to find his room empty.

Even as alarm jolted through him, his gaze snagged on the green and striped clothing discarded on the bathroom floor. His own clothes were abandoned on the foot of his bed.

He strode toward the phone on the night table, planning to ask the doorman if a naked woman had walked through the lobby, when he spied the bottom of her bare foot resting on the arm of the love seat that faced the windows. He peered over the back and found her fast asleep, arm curled under the cushion she'd pulled under her ear.

She didn't look as young now that she was out of her costume and her clownish makeup was washed away. Her cheekbones were high and well-defined, her mouth relaxed and somber. Her skin was so smooth and fine-grained, he wanted to touch her cheek, but he was torn over whether to wake her.

Patience wasn't one of his virtues. Virtues weren't really among his virtues. He abided by the law and treated people with civility, but he wasn't trying to prove anything to anyone. He didn't believe in heaven so he didn't strive to get there.

But he didn't needlessly torture people when they were at the end of their rope, either. He wanted to know how she came to be working a dead-end job that left her so exhausted she passed out before dinner, but he let her sleep.

And, not for the first time, wondered if she might be taking drugs.

He took the decorative throw off the back of the love seat and draped it over her, then went downstairs to shamelessly go through the pockets of her coat. He came up with a handful of loose change, a subway card, a lip balm, a broken candy cane and a set of two keys, likely for an apartment door and a mailbox.

He sat down to eat alone—which wasn't unusual for him. It was, however, the first time in a long time that he wished he could call Ilias. Not that Konstantin had ever called him. No, Ilias had reached out so often Konstantin had rarely placed the call himself.

Ilias had been Konstantin's friend whether he had wanted one or not. He hadn't. Friendship had been an unfamiliar concept to him. Konstantin hadn't had siblings and had rarely seen children his own age before he'd been plucked from his father's remote farm and thrust into his grandfather's lavish world.

But Konstantin had no sooner got used to the cavernous mansion outside Athens when his grandfather had sent him to "get a proper education."

At ten years old, he had found himself in a rainy English autumn, unable to speak a word of the language, surrounded by boys who all seemed to know each other, or have common interests, or understand how things were done.

It had been a nightmare. Konstantin understood how to be alone and preferred it. He had tried to seek solitude at every opportunity, but Ilias had said, *We're the only two Greeks in our year. We have to stick together.*

Ilias already spoke English he'd learned from his mother.

He was outgoing, quick-witted and so personable, even Konstantin couldn't hate him.

By contrast, one of the first words Konstantin had learned was *sullen*.

Why so sullen, Master Galanis? the teacher had mocked, making the entire room of boys laugh at him.

He'd been sullen because he'd been cold and miserable and bewildered. He'd never had proper schooling, only what his mother had managed to teach him. Even the basics of math and reading in Greek were difficult for him, but Ilias had sat with him for countless hours, teaching him to draw the letters, tutoring him and helping him finish his homework.

Half the time, Ilias would say, *Just copy mine so we can go play football.* But the end result was that Konstantin had kept up and passed all his exams. He had also learned there was at least one person in this world who had his back.

Aside from those first couple of years when they'd both been homesick for Greece, Konstantin had never understood what Ilias saw in him. Konstantin would sometimes kick a football or walk to the shops if it was only him and Ilias, but he had little desire to spend time with anyone else. The rest of the boys and their mindless pursuits were superficial and immature.

Ilias would seek him out, though, especially after talking to his mother. Ilias's father had died when he was six and his mother had only relinquished him to boarding school because it was the school Ilias's father had gone to. It had been his father's wish that his son attend it, too. His mother had seemed to need a lot of connection with her son, calling nearly daily from wherever she happened to be, needing advice and reassurance. Ilias was always patient with her, but after ending the call, he would seem quietly distressed.

Konstantin had never known what to do with that. He understood the pressure of responsibility if not the weight of emotion that Ilias seemed to carry. The other boys would cajole Ilias to "cheer up!" but he would dismiss them, then ask Konstantin if he wanted to study. Over time, Konstantin had concluded it was the very fact that he *didn't* ask anything of Ilias that made Ilias gravitate to him.

When their university years arrived, they took different directions. Konstantin went to Oxford while Ilias went to Harvard, then Konstantin had to cut his education short. His grandfather had become ill and left such a financial mess of the shipping business, Konstantin had had to step in to right it.

By then, Konstantin had lived half his life in poverty, and the second half in luxury. He knew which lifestyle he preferred. He'd been prepared to grind himself to the bone to keep the company afloat and keep himself in the comforts of wealth.

To his shock, Ilias had not only learned what he was up against, he had stepped in with a loan, completely unasked, leveraging the trust fund he'd gained access to at twenty-one. That had given Konstantin enough breathing room to make swift, radical changes that had been risky, but had not only saved his grandfather's company, but doubled its share value within two years.

At that point, investors had lined up to throw money at him. They liked having young ambitious blood at the helm.

Konstantin had been growing the company ever since, expanding into tech, commodities, green energy and anything else he thought could turn a profit.

When he had repaid his loan to Ilias, with suitable interest, Konstantin had gone to the US to arrange it. By then, Ilias had been finished at Harvard and was living in New

York, beginning his career as an architect. It had been December. The streets and pubs and shops had been bustling with crowds, but Ilias had dragged Konstantin into all of those places.

"Mother has a new boyfriend. She's spending Christmas with him at his castle in Scotland. Eloise would rather come here. You should stay and spend the holidays with us."

Konstantin had been introduced to Ilias's little sister through toothless photos and clumsy drawings that had arrived at school in the mail. Occasionally, he had eavesdropped on conversations over the tablet when she had plonked her way through a piano lesson or complained about something at school. She was eight years younger than they were so she'd always been very much a child, especially once he had left school to work and she was still wearing braces and pigtails.

He didn't dislike her, but the invitation reeked of sentimentality. He had never celebrated any winter holiday, not beyond a quiet meal with his grandfather who had been gone for three years by then.

Nevertheless, out of respect for his friend and the enormous financial favor Ilias had done him, Konstantin had stuck around.

He barely recognized Eloise when he saw her. She had never looked much like her brother. They had different fathers, but she was no longer a child. She was seventeen and looking chic in snug jeans and a turtleneck. Her hair had been cut as short as his own, revealing her ears and nape. Her green-gold eyes and wide mouth dominated her otherwise delicate face.

Konstantin hadn't known what to say to her, but the siblings had bantered enough that it wasn't noticed. As Ilias started to pour drinks, they had argued over who had finished the last of the eggnog and who would pick up more. Ilias refused to let her go.

"I'd like a rum and eggnog today, thank you. If you go, you'll be gone for hours, chatting with everyone in the store. I don't need to know the bodega operator's hobbies or how many kittens the neighbor's cat had. No. You asked for a tree. You stay here and decorate it." He pointed at the fragrant evergreen.

"This from the man who can't get a coffee without getting a number," she lobbed back.

"Good luck with this one." Ilias thumbed over his shoulder with mock disgust on his way out the door. "I may or may not come back."

Konstantin had tried to ignore Eloise, but she did like to chat. Before he'd known it, she had corralled him into helping decorate the tree. As they'd stood close and their fingers had brushed and she looked up at him, he'd been struck by the woman she was on her way to becoming. He'd *seen* her.

And he'd wanted her.

That sudden rush of masculine energy had been so far offside he'd stepped *way* back. So far back he'd left the apartment and flown to Athens that night.

Ilias had been surprised by his abrupt departure and Konstantin had blamed Eloise's childhood case of hero worship, which had never actually bothered him, always seeming harmless. In those moments beside the tree, however, he'd seen her attraction to him. He wasn't flattering himself. He was a healthy, wealthy man. Women had been noticing him for years. He damned well knew what mutual attraction was and feeling it with her had sent him into a mental fishtail.

So he left, and Konstantin had never seen Ilias in person

again. He hadn't seen Eloise until the news had reached him that Ilias had been killed in a small plane crash.

He never looked back if he could avoid it and didn't let himself dwell on those nightmarish days now. He had done what he could for Ilias and his family, but it had been pure hell. The funeral service, the eulogy, had been like driving his car into a brick wall at full speed. He had made himself do it, but the impact had nearly destroyed him. Especially when he looked at Eloise.

The agony in her eyes had nearly broken him in two. He hadn't known what to say, how to mitigate the vastness of loss she was experiencing. He would fall into it himself if he tried. He'd had a near irresistible urge to take her away from all of this. To somehow pull her behind the wall he used to buffer himself from pain.

Don't feel anything, he silently urged her. *Don't suffer.*

She had been glued to her mother's side, steel to Lilja's shattered glass. There had been people everywhere, all wanting to approach mother and sister, to condole with them. Ilias had always been popular.

It had been winter again. An Athens winter, but still cold. At the reception after the service, Konstantin had stood outside in the bite of weather, done with old faces from school who he'd never liked in the first place. Done with small talk. Done with the sheer brutality of life.

But he couldn't make himself leave.

Then, as the light faded, Eloise had found him in the garden. She'd been a shadow of herself. Her black dress had made her look shapeless and washed out. She'd struck him as translucent. Brittle as a sculpture made of ice.

He remembered wanting to warm her. *Needing* to hold her. Then, somehow, his mouth was on hers and light burst forth inside him, gusting into a furnace of heat. She had tasted like salvation. Like purpose and hope and the future.

She hadn't pushed him away. Her arm had curled tighter behind his neck.

That was small comfort. What kind of man *did* that to a grieving woman? Especially one who was still too young for him?

He had pushed her away and he pushed from the table now, stalking across the room to get away from a kiss that had only happened because his self-discipline had been smashed by loss. He'd been too disgusted with himself afterward to reach out to her.

He had told her to contact him if she needed anything, but he hadn't been surprised when she never did. She and her mother had been surrounded by support that day. That's how it had looked, anyway.

Now he had to wonder.

Everything in him was wondering about her. Wondering in that way that went well beyond polite interest in an old friend's kid sister.

She wasn't a kid any longer. She was at least twenty-four. Her blush of awareness when he had asked if she wanted a bath, and the way her lashes had flickered as her gaze swept over him, had signaled she was still attracted to him.

An answering interest was gripping him, sharp and barbed.

He tightened his hand around his glass, resisting this involuntary reaction. It was carnal and human, but still misplaced. She was Ilias's little sister. She was on her back foot and needed help.

She was still off-limits.

He tilted his glass to let scotch bite his tongue.

CHAPTER FOUR

ELOISE WOKE DISORIENTED, thinking she was still dreaming because she was flying through the snow falling over the city. No. Those buildings were real. She was—

She sat up with a startled gasp, catching at the blanket before it slipped to the floor, but it was only the robe falling open across her bare legs. Her head swam as she stood to retie the belt and get her head on straight.

Through the predawn light, she saw the shape of someone in the bed.

Oh, no.

Her insides writhed with discomfiture at falling asleep in the first place, then sharing the room all night with Konstantin. It felt intimate, but also provocative. Did he sleep naked?

Don't.

She had to leave.

She tiptoed to the bathroom, planning to dress and slip away, but he spoke in a graveled voice muffled by the pillow.

"We don't have to get up for another hour. Do you want to sleep in a real bed?"

"No." Her voice hit a note that should have shattered the windows.

"There's one down the hall," he clarified.

Oh. Of course, he wouldn't invite her into his. Thank goodness it was barely light, not that he was looking at her to see the stinging heat that rushed into her cheeks.

"I'm fine. Go back to sleep." She went into the bathroom and closed the door before she turned on the light. Her elf uniform wasn't here. Neither were the clothes he'd loaned her.

She cracked the door to whisper, "Where are my clothes?"

"I threw them out."

"*Why?*"

"We're doing this now, then?" The blankets rustled as he rolled over, then they fell down his chest as his bent arms came up and flexed.

Dangerous tendrils of intrigue curled through her belly. "Doing what?" Her voice was still too high.

"Getting up. Talking."

"No. I'm going home."

With an impatient sigh, Konstantin threw back the covers and rose.

The winter light cast his bare chest and muscled legs in shades of pewter. He wore boxer briefs in a slash of black across his hips, but a jolt still went through her as she confronted all that naked skin. His physique was lean and powerful enough to dry her mouth.

And was he—?

She yanked her gaze to the windows, trying to unsee the press of his morning wood against his underwear.

"Did you take something?" he asked briskly.

"What?" She glanced to see he was dressing in the clothes she'd left on the foot of the bed. He had the track pants over his hips and yanked the drawstring before he tied it off.

"Drugs. Is that why you passed out?"

"*No.* I already told you I don't take drugs."

"Are you ill? Pregnant?"

"What on earth do you think I'm doing with my life? No. I've been working two jobs. I was tired." She looked to the door, thinking she'd have to go home in just her coat. It would look like the ultimate walk of shame, which it kind of was, but it was hardly the worst outfit on the subway on a Wednesday morning.

"I found an all-night boutique and had them deliver something closer to your size." He bent and snagged a massive shopping bag from the floor. He plopped it on the bench at the foot of the bed.

"That—" She couldn't really claim it wasn't necessary, could she? "Thank you."

"Come downstairs when you're dressed." He walked out, pulling the T-shirt over his head as he went.

She wavered briefly, then carried the oversized bag into the bathroom where she sifted through her options.

Drugs? Really? She was too broke to be anything but stone-cold sober.

She shook out a pair of jeans and looked at the selection of tops. There were a couple of plain T-shirts, a waffle-knit sweatshirt and a fuzzy blue cardigan along with fresh undies and bright pink socks.

The jeans were loose and she had to turn up the cuffs, but they were better than wearing anything of his. The layered tops hugged her comfortingly and the fuzzy cardigan was almost as snuggly as the robe had been.

Her hair was a disaster, given she'd slept on it wet before fully combing it out. It was flattened to one side and the part felt wrong, but she mostly wore it in a ponytail or a bun these days. Did the man own anything resembling a hair tie, though? Of course not.

She dampened her hair, combed it, then tucked it behind her ears and turned away in disgust.

When she got downstairs, Konstantin was speaking to a middle-aged woman who was setting two places on the end of the long dining table. The T-shirt shifted and hugged his muscled shoulders as he poured himself a coffee. His biceps bulged below the short sleeves. His feet were bare.

Eloise faltered, trying not to be mesmerized. She had only come this far to say goodbye, but the aroma of waffles and bacon and fresh coffee hit her nostrils, making her stomach cramp with hunger.

She hadn't had a lot of time to sleep these days and even less for eating.

"You missed dinner. Sit," Konstantin said, then dismissed his housekeeper with the news that, "We'll be gone by nine. Come back then and close the apartment. I'll email in the New Year to let you know when I'll be back. Enjoy your vacation."

"Thank you." The woman nodded and sent a pleasant smile toward Eloise on her way through the door beside the pantry.

This was quite a feast to be thrown together at the last minute. His housekeeper must have known Konstantin was expecting company this morning.

Unjustified jealousy twinged through Eloise at the thought of him sharing his wide bed with Gemma Wilkinson, then coming down here to play footsie while they ate breakfast.

Konstantin held a chair to the right of his spot at the head of the table. "Tell me how you've come to this."

The meal was too tempting. She sank into the chair and spooned berries from the different dishes onto her waffle, topped it with a drizzle of strawberry syrup, then added a dollop of whipped cream.

Konstantin sat and leaned to fill her cup with coffee, extending his tanned arm across her line of vision. How could the sight of an arm cause sizzling heat to climb from the pit of her belly up her lower back, across her chest and into her neck? It was ridiculous!

She slid a crispy morsel of waffle into her mouth, putting off answering because she felt so stupid about being here like this.

"Mmm…" The sweet flavors exploded on her tongue along with the burst of berries and the fluffy texture of the whipped cream. She closed her eyes to savor it.

When she opened her eyes, Konstantin was watching her intently. Her heart flip-flopped and a fresh blush flooded with a sting into her cheeks.

She forced herself to swallow, but where to start?

Maybe if she hadn't been so entitled in the first place, taking food like this for granted? Maybe if she'd taken better care of herself and not been so oblivious and selfish?

Her descent into this predicament was intensely painful to look at and admit to, but at least he would understand how it started.

"Things were difficult after Ilias." She cleared her throat with a sip of coffee. It was a dark roast, bitter and delicious and piping hot. "Mom has had a lot of loss in her life and losing people isn't something anyone could get used to. She's always been on the sensitive side, anyway. Emotionally, I mean. She feels things very deeply."

She glanced up, not wanting him to think she was bad-mouthing her mother or judging Lilja. Her mother's personality tended toward codependent. That was just reality.

He was listening intently. His condensed attention made her feel as though she had a lens on herself that amplified everything, making her ultra self-conscious.

"I was trying to be strong for her, the way Ilias had always been. I didn't realize how badly I was taking his being gone until I went back to university. Mom had started seeing someone so I thought I was ready to resume my life, too. I wound up staying in my room for an entire semester."

Konstantin's brows crashed together. "No one helped you? Schoolmates?"

"I didn't have any. I'd only been there for a couple of months when it happened, then I was gone for more than a year. The few friends I'd made were doing their own things." Partying, studying, dating and traveling. "Eventually, I got myself back into the lecture halls, but my interest wasn't there. I was failing out of classes, couldn't settle on a major. Mom still needed a lot of support. She likes to have a man in her life and she loves to talk about it when she does." Eloise found a wry smile, but it slid straight off her mouth because she should have been paying closer attention during that time. "I've always found it better to distance myself when she's dating someone new so I stayed at uni, trying to find my way."

"Why is it better to distance yourself?" His eyes narrowed inquisitively.

Men were so naive sometimes. She hesitated, but the reason men were naive was because women hated talking about it.

"Growing up, there were times when the man she was dating viewed us as a two-for-one deal," she admitted flatly.

"Lilja put up with that?" His voice thickened with outrage.

"Of course not. She always got rid of them immediately."

"How did it happen more than once? Did Ilias know?" he demanded.

"Sometimes. Don't look at me like that," she said of his accusatory glower. "It was hard enough telling my mother that her beau had grabbed my butt or tried to kiss me on the lips. I didn't want to repeat it to my brother. She always dealt with it and I learned to keep out of the way."

"This is unbelievable." He scraped his chair back and rose to pace near the window.

"You think I'm *lying*?"

"No," he barked over his shoulder. "I'm reminded of the depths some of my sex will sink to and I'm sickened by it. I just can't believe…" He pinched the bridge of his nose.

"Don't judge Mom too harshly," she said into the silence. "Her happiest time in life was when she was married to Ilias's father. She's been looking for that ever since. It's not her fault that some of the men she kissed turned out to be toads. The fault is mine for letting her marry one. Although, I think one of the reasons she liked Antoine so much is that he's always taken this very paternal attitude toward me instead of, you know, being overly friendly."

Konstantin turned, arms folded across his powerful chest. "What's his last name again?"

"Rousseau?"

He shrugged. "It wasn't familiar to me when she married him, but… He's no good?"

She dipped a strawberry in whipped cream and ate it, trying to sweeten the bitterness that had landed on her tongue.

"At first, he seemed like the answer to my prayers. Mom had known him for years and she had always found him charming."

Konstantin's brows went up in speculation.

She nodded grimly. "Given what I know of him now, I can't help thinking he'd kept a hook baited for her. He gave her what she was looking for, though. He romanced her and he's very attentive, pampers her and placates her moods. Once she started seeing him, she called me less often. When I did talk to her, she sounded calmer and happier. You don't realize how badly you need a full night's sleep until you get one, you know? Kind of like today," she joked, glancing up again.

His expression remained stony. She looked back to her plate.

"Mom always said she wouldn't remarry unless she was in love so when they got engaged, I thought it was the real deal. She was excited for the wedding and the honeymoon. He was always a gentleman around me, even though he was always *there*."

"What do you mean?"

"At first, I thought he was just trying to, you know, bond with his wife's daughter. But he made it impossible for me to get Mom alone for more than five minutes. He was constantly inserting himself, driving the conversation where he wanted it to go. Or didn't want it to go. Part of me thought, who cares? *I'm* not married to him. He makes her happy." She braced her elbows on the table and covered the shame that creased her face. "I hate myself so much for being *relieved* that she was leaning on him instead of me."

"She used to do that with Ilias."

"She did," she agreed, picking up her head. "I really took him for granted that way. I took a lot of things for granted," she muttered as she gathered her cutlery again, but her appetite was muted by remorse. "Anyway, having that breathing space gave me a chance see that I hadn't been taking care of myself. I finally began thinking about what I wanted to do with my life."

"That's when you began your excursion to the North Pole?"

"Ha-ha. No. Ilias had always told me I should work in music. I'm not orchestra-level talent, but I wound up talking to a grief counselor who used music therapy. I realized that was something that interested me. The problem was, I'd already failed out of two universities. None of those classes really transferred, anyway. I found a program here in New York that accepted me, but when it came time to pay tuition and look for an apartment, Antoine refused to pay for any of it."

"*Antoine* did." A deep note entered Konstantin's voice that was lethal enough to make her skin prickle.

"Yes. Mom had always used a trustee to manage her fortune. Cyrus. When he retired, Antoine took over. It's totally within Mom's right to let him. It's her money from her first husband."

"None came from your father?"

"No." A small pang of mixed feelings struck, those that reminded her she wasn't really a Drakos, merely a product of her mother's whimsical appreciation for a good-looking man. "My father was a professional surfer. He made enough to stay on the circuit, but he had a bohemian personality. He died when I was five. I don't really remember him."

"What did your mother say about Antoine cutting you off?"

"Nothing." She got another bite of waffle into her mouth and chewed, but all her enjoyment was gone. "Given the history between us when it came to men, I didn't want to get between her and her husband. And Antoine had a point. It had always been on Mom to support me. I'm an adult and she doesn't owe me a penny. She had already given me four years of university and I had nothing to show for it. I accept all of that, but..."

"Surely, Ilias made arrangements for you."

"He didn't expect to die before he was thirty, did he?"

"That shouldn't have happened," Konstantin said with muted fury, looking toward the window where snow swirled beyond the glass. "I ask myself daily if I should have talked him out of taking those lessons. He always seemed so competent."

"He was. And he had a qualified pilot with him." Bird strikes didn't always take down a plane, but in this case, it had. "We met with lawyers once the funeral was over, obviously, but all of that is a blur to me."

At the mention of the funeral, Konstantin flashed his attention back to her. His delving look caused that strange pull in her belly.

She looked down at her plate, not wanting him to know how many times she'd relived their kiss. How much it had confused her and left her incapable of fully tracking what had happened those immediate days after, when they'd been trying to chart the path forward.

She rubbed her brow.

"I remember Cyrus saying there were sufficient funds for my schooling, but I don't remember how much. Control of the Drakos fortune reverted to Mom and I'm almost certain they said I would become a cotrustee if something happened to her. At the time, she just handed everything back to Cyrus. He had managed it before Ilias was old enough to do it and when I emailed *him* to say I was ready to go back to school, he took care of all my bills. I'm embarrassed to say that's all that mattered to me at the time. Then Cyrus retired and Antoine got his tentacles in."

"You're still her daughter. Does she know you're living like this? Surely, she wants you to be safe?"

"Safely married," she said dryly. "Antoine is very persuasive. He's got her convinced that I should marry Edoardo Ricci. You might know the banking family?"

"He's too old for you." His words lashed like a whip across the room.

"He's thirty-three," she said with a snort. "One year older than you."

His cheek ticked, but he didn't insist *he* was too old for her.

"Do you want to marry him?" he asked gruffly instead.

"No. Otherwise, I'd be there, getting married, wouldn't I? Not that there's anything wrong with him." Beyond the fact he wasn't Konstantin. She looked into her coffee. "I think about giving in every day. I know it would ease Mom's mind if I was settled. She would love to plan a wedding," she said into her cup, sipping to wet her damp throat. "But I find Antoine so patronizing. He said there was no point in Mom paying for my education if I'm only going to be a wife and mother, anyway. He said I've been enough of a drain on her resources and it's time that I..." She looked to the ceiling, still galled. "That I *contribute to the family fortunes in a constructive manner.*"

"That implies *he* has contributed to her fortune in some way. Has he?"

"I don't know. He has money from a previous marriage, I think." She hated the sound of Antoine's voice so she rarely listened to it. "Anyway, I told him to get stuffed, that I was going to school and walked out. I admit I was behaving like a spoiled brat. I flew here to look for an apartment, thinking he would cool off and go back to paying my bills. I thought Mom would insist on it. I've *always* had an allowance."

She massaged the tension that invaded her brow again, unable to look at him because she was so embarrassed by that sense of entitlement.

"Maybe I deserved to be brought down a peg, but as soon as I landed, he cut off my credit cards and bricked my phone. I had to sell what jewelry I had on me to pay my hotel bill. When I finally got hold of Mom, Antoine was right there saying that if I wanted to come back and continue talking about Edoardo, he would send me a plane ticket. I said no thanks and hung up. I've been here, living on spite, ever since."

He didn't laugh. "When was this?"

"April."

"What does Lilja think you've been doing all this time?"

"Going to school. When I said it, I was planning to get a student loan, but it felt like too big a hole to dig myself into. I kept up the lie as an excuse for not going home. I don't want Antoine to know he has my back against a wall."

"And your only income is door-to-door sales?"

"It's not—no. I serve breakfast at a trattoria on Fifth Avenue." She'd been crying into her espresso when the server had mentioned they were looking for help. "I room with one of my coworkers. She gets the more lucrative dinner shifts, but even the tips from a coffee and croissant are good. So were the tips from the Twelve Days gig. One of the dads gave me fifty dollars the first night. I was like, dude. Pace yourself. There are eleven more deliveries to go." *So much for* that *cash cow*, she thought wistfully.

"This is not what Ilias would want for you."

"Neither is marriage to a stranger. He wouldn't want Mom at the mercy of someone like Antoine, either. I feel *horrible* for that." The guilt ate at her constantly.

"Antoine took advantage of both of you. I'll step in. Straighten things out."

"How?" Her heart nearly came out her throat. "No. Don't get involved." It killed her to say it but, "I'm finally connected to Mom again. It's only a few texts and Antoine listens to all our calls, but if you go stirring the pot, he'll cut me off again. *No.* Thank you," she added in a shaken voice. "Stay out of it."

"He has no right to prevent you from speaking to your mother."

His lash of cold temper was... She wasn't sure. He was outraged on her behalf, which was heartening, but it seemed deeper and broader and more personal than it warranted. She didn't know how to interpret the cold malevolence that seemed to radiate from him. It made her cautious as she tried to defend her position.

"She thinks she loves him. He seems to love her back. What are you going to do? Shatter her beliefs and force her to suffer yet another heartbreak? I've caused her to lose men before."

"Men who didn't deserve to be with her," he pointed out with a flash of temper.

"Sure, but it would still be my fault. Again." Eloise had been down that road. Maybe her mother wouldn't hold a grudge, but it would still be painful and awful. "No. I appreciate the sympathetic ear and the hot meal, but I have everything under control."

That was such a lie that she couldn't look at him as she said it.

His snort told her he didn't buy it, either.

She stabbed at her waffle, focusing on finishing her breakfast so he wouldn't see the shadows of hopelessness in her eyes.

* * *

Konstantin retook his seat, resuming his breakfast while he filtered through the various avenues of inquiry he would take to correct for his failure to ensure Eloise and her mother were properly taken care of after Ilias had passed.

How had he thought they would be okay? That had been so shortsighted on his part; he was beyond disgusted with himself.

"What sorts of things have you been up to since, um…" Eloise's voice broke into his concentration, but then she seemed to realize that "since I saw you last" was a reference to the funeral and their kiss. "Lately," she mumbled and closed her lips over her fork.

Why was she engaging in inane small talk?

"Is that too personal?" Wariness edged into her expression. "I was only trying to make conversation."

"My life never changes. Work keeps me busy. I like it that way."

"But you're seeing, um… She's the actress, right? I'm really sorry about your date last night. I feel like I should apologize to her."

She sounded like Ilias, voice soaked with empathy for a complete stranger, wanting everyone to get along and willing to pave the way with their own beating heart if necessary.

"That's over. Forget it." He shrugged it away.

"The relationship is over? Or…?" Eloise searched his eyes as though delving for truth. For *feelings*. "Or do you mean you've made up with her and it's all okay?"

"I'm not in the habit of discussing my personal life," he reminded her.

Her expression went blank, proving she was even more sensitive than Ilias had ever been because he'd hurt her feelings. It brought out an agitation in Konstantin that wanted to bark, *For God's sake, protect yourself.*

Especially from me, was the follow-up thought.

He'd been hardened off very early in life while she had been raised by a high-needs mother who had left her so emotionally drained she'd neglected herself after suffering a devastating blow. Now she was being put through the wringer by her stepfather.

Guilt twisted like a knife behind his navel. That was more his fault than hers. He knew it even if she didn't.

"The relationship wasn't serious. Now it's over," he clarified for no particular reason except that he wanted her to know it. He refused to pick apart why. His cup went into its saucer with a click. "I sent flowers and something she could exchange at Tiffany's."

Her faint nod frustrated him for some inexplicable reason. Because she was judging him? No, he decided. It was the situation that was eating at him.

"Ilias would have paid your tuition and supported you through your education—"

"Please don't." She put up a hand, sounding appalled. "I didn't come here expecting anything more than a friendly catch up."

"Why is that?"

"Because we're strangers," she stated. "You don't owe me anything."

Like hell. He rejected that remark at such a base level he was insulted she would even say it aloud.

"Ilias bailed out my grandfather's company when we were still at university. Did you know that?"

"No. I mean, I remember him saying you had to quit school early because your grandfather was ill. And I know that you came to New York that time because you were squaring up with him on some old business." A blush crept into her cheeks and her gaze skittered away from his as she referenced that day by the Christmas tree. "Ilias never implied it was a big deal, though."

"It was a very big deal." Konstantin tried to ignore the sexual awareness that ignited within him each time he saw her react to him. "My grandfather became ill and I wasn't fully prepared to take over. Things were a mess. Vultures were circling. If not for Ilias, I would have lost everything."

"I doubt that." A smile flickered across her lips. "He always spoke about you as being very intelligent and ambitious. He admired you."

Konstantin couldn't help a reflexive frown at that, not caring for the pitch of emotion it caused within him: pain, loss, *more* guilt that he had ignored his obligations to Ilias's family.

"The point I'm making is that I remain in his debt." He was embarrassed that he had allowed himself to believe that paying off the financial side of things had been enough.

Eloise regarded him solemnly. "Ilias was never one to keep a score sheet. You know that."

"But he had a strong sense of right and wrong. What is happening to you is wrong." It made him livid.

It didn't sound as though Antoine was violent, the way Konstantin's father had been, but his controlling, bullyish behavior was all too familiar. And Antoine's neglect of Eloise looked an awful lot like the way his own grandfather had ignored his daughter's plight, leaving her in the hands of a monster.

"If Ilias were alive today, you would be well taken care of." Konstantin had no doubt in that. "What if something happens to your mother? Who inherits the Drakos fortune? *Antoine*?"

"Probably." She sighed as though that were something she couldn't bear thinking about. Then she sent him a beseeching look. "This isn't about the money, though. I honestly don't care if I have to work grubby jobs and live with a roommate. I need my mother in my life. She's all I have. I don't want to hurt her, or see her hurt, or get hurt myself. And I don't see any way that I can intervene in her marriage without that happening."

"So you intend to continue tolerating this?"

"What are my options?" She threw up her hands. "Either she stays with a man who wants to push me to the periphery of her life, or I start a war with him that tears Mom and meI apart, anyway. How would I even go about extricating him? Claim that she wasn't competent when she put him in charge? He's her husband. Calling her state of mind into question would only bolster his position as custodian of her money. Even if I somehow pried him from her life, then what? I'm the one who broke up her relationships *again*. Believe me, I spend every day trying to find a good way out of this and there is none."

"I don't accept that." He understood that relationships could be complicated. It was another reason he avoided them, but it was very clear to him that he couldn't allow things to go on as they were. "I'll take you to Nice. I want to meet this man."

"Why? There's no point," she protested.

"There are many points. You want to see your mother, don't you? For Christmas?"

"That's so unfair, it's cruel," she said with a wounded pang in her voice. "Of course, I want to see her. But she already told me she's going away. Antoine booked it," she added sullenly. "I think he did it to keep me from asking to come home, but maybe I'm being paranoid."

"Where are they going?"

"Como, I think. It's a house party. They're leaving after their own party on Friday."

"Which means she's in Nice until Friday. Come with me or don't, but I intend to see for myself what kind of situation she's in."

"I can't—I have to work my shift." She sent an anxious look at the clock. "I can't leave town without covering my share of rent. My roommate will get kicked out and it will be my fault."

"Your sense of responsibility would be commendable, Eloise, if you weren't clinging to such a sinking ship. Please," he said with deep irony. "Since it's my fault you lost your job, allow me to cover your rent."

CHAPTER FIVE

BY THE TIME they were buckled into Konstantin's private jet, Eloise's roommate was sending her every Christmas emoji and a text.

Why did he send so much? Aren't you coming back?

Eloise had run into their apartment to grab her passport and a quick bag to travel, but her roommate hadn't been home. She'd been called to the trattoria to cover the shift Eloise was missing. Now she was fired from that job, too.

"How much did you send her?" Eloise asked Konstantin, looking up from her phone.

"A year's worth."

"Because it's Christmas?"

"Because you're not going back there. Even before I saw the building, I knew by the rent that those are squalid living conditions. Tell her to use it to find a better address along with a new roommate."

If they weren't already taxiing along the runway, Eloise might have staged more of a rebellion. As it was, she could only relay exactly what he had said, mostly because she didn't know how she would get back to New York, let alone pay rent again when she did.

She didn't know what would happen when she arrived

in Nice. If it were up to her mother, Eloise would be invited to move back into the house, but Lilja had bought it with Antoine. He wasn't likely to allow Eloise to stay overnight, let alone through Christmas.

She glanced at Konstantin, so effortlessly sophisticated and compelling. He'd shaved and changed into a black turtleneck with a casual fawn-colored jacket. His dark brown trousers were tailored to graze perfectly across his polished ankle boots.

He looked up from his phone and caught her staring at him.

"Where…um…?" She cleared her throat. "Last night you said you were leaving town today. Where were you supposed to go?"

"The Maldives."

"Oh? Do you have property there?"

"No."

"Just vacation, then?"

"Yes."

"With…um…" She adjusted her blind as though there were something to see outside the window beyond a wall of white clouds.

"Yes," he said before she finished asking if he'd been planning to take Gemma.

Maybe it was better that he wasn't a talkative person.

"Have you told your mother that we're coming?" he asked.

"Not yet." She picked up her phone again.

"Don't mention me. I'd like the element of surprise."

She was still uneasy about all of this, worried about what he might say or do when he saw her mother again. She chewed her lip as she considered what to say, then spoke as she typed out her text.

·"I'm arriving in Nice late tonight." She tried to go down a line and accidentally hit Send. "Argh, this phone. Let me know… Tsk… Give me a sec."

While she cleared the garbled letters, her mother's response came through.

"Where are you staying? With friends or at a hotel?" she read aloud. "That has to be Antoine replying."

"He takes her phone?"

"I think he must. And I think he deletes anything he doesn't want her to see. When I talk to her, she always asks when I'm coming to visit. Then one time I said why don't you come see me in New York and suddenly Antoine wanted to take her to Australia." She tried to keep the pain of rejection off her face, but Konstantin had to see it.

"Just say both," he instructed.

That she was staying with a friend at a hotel? She didn't want to be even more indebted to him, but had no choice. She stifled her protest and texted.

Both. Let me know when it would be convenient to drop in.

"I'm invited to lunch tomorrow," she conveyed a moment later, mollified as her mother's invitation came through.

See you then.

She typed her reply and touched it to Send. It didn't go, making her sigh. She rubbed the screen on her thigh before trying again. Finally, it whooshed.

"Honestly, half the reason I can't stay in touch with her is this stupid phone."

"What's wrong with it?" He frowned.

"It's just old. And the screen is cracked. I swapped my

good one with my roommate for rent the first month. It works well enough for texting, which is really all I need. Definitely no photos, though. The poor thing goes into a sulk and I have to put it down for a nap before it will work again."

"Do you even have my number? Is that why you never called me?"

"I'm sure I do somewhere, but I wouldn't have called it." She tucked her phone away and turned her eyes to the window.

"Why not?" he asked in a dangerous growl.

"Because..." She winced, hating to offer up the last of her dignity, but his tone demanded an answer. "In those first weeks after arriving in New York, when I realized Antoine was playing hard ball, I reached out to some people I knew, friends who had apartments. One let me stay with her for a few days, but Antoine wasn't coming around and I was very broke. That stinks worse than old fish. I quickly got the message that if I wasn't able to drop everything to fly to Turks and Caicos, if I needed a *job,* then I didn't belong in their world. That stung enough that I didn't want to risk getting the same treatment from anyone else." Especially him.

"You presumed I'm as shallow as they are?"

"I didn't know how you would react. I barely know you." How were they still in the clouds and not above them?

"You keep saying that." He sounded aggravated.

"Because it's true," she said with an ironic quirk of her mouth. "You're a private person. Remember?" She was sorry she'd brought it up as soon as she said it. She hurried to add, "The fact is, Antoine had a point. I needed to grow up and quit expecting other people to take care of me." She made herself meet his gaze, even though it was hard to hold his flinty look. "I miss Mom and I *really* appreciate you taking me home to see her, but you honestly don't owe me anything. Carry on to your vacation tomorrow."

He narrowed his eyes and looked as though he were ready to say something, but the flight attendant came to ask if they wanted breakfast. They'd only eaten two hours ago so Eloise declined, but she asked the woman how she could watch a movie, purely to put an end to this charged conversation.

Konstantin spent the rest of the flight working while Eloise moved to the sofa and put on noise-canceling headphones to watch movies.

He shouldn't have been distracted by her. She sat quietly with a blanket across her lap, absorbed in Christmas-themed storylines with heavily decorated sets, women in garishly bedecked pullovers and handymen who held hammers but never swung them. Every time he looked up, there seemed to be an impromptu kiss in front of a glowing tree.

He rarely watched movies. Work relaxed him. There was something about making decisions and taking action that powered him up. A dopamine rush, he supposed. And the triumph in arriving at a peak that put him that much further from the rock bottom he'd been born into.

After a while, Eloise drifted off again. He wasn't surprised. The low stakes and cozy fires on the screen were enough to put him into a coma, but it reminded him how rundown she was.

He almost sent another email to his assistant, asking for a doctor to give her a medical checkup, but he had already overloaded the young man with research requests on Antoine.

He was actually leaning on his executive assistant's assistant. His EA was on vacation because Konstantin had expected to be on vacation himself. Everything slowed down at this time of year, forcing him to do the same, but Konstantin found vacation very boring. He usually continued working and the junior assistant stuck around the office to remotely pull reports or pass along messages.

It didn't take a psychologist to work out that Konstantin preferred to keep his brain busy so he could avoid his emotions, and that he was leaping on Eloise as a project so he could sidestep the more volatile guilt of letting down his friend and the shame of seeing his friend's sister through a carnal lens.

You don't owe me anything, she had claimed, but he damned well did.

He owed Ilias, but it went deeper than that. When Eloise had said that she hadn't wanted to risk Konstantin rejecting her request for help, he'd suffered a deep sting of culpability, as though he *had* rejected her.

Hadn't he, though? It was far too similar to the way his grandfather had stayed deliberately ignorant to what was happening to Konstantin and his mother. He could remember her pleading with the old man on the phone, after they'd walked all the way into the village.

Please, Baba. Please let me come home.

The old man had been unmoved by her regret in her marriage. She'd gone against his wishes and gotten herself pregnant, hadn't she? She would have to lie in the bed she'd made.

Konstantin couldn't help feeling he'd been just as heartless in not staying in touch. That infernal, misplaced kiss had stopped him. If he saw her again, he'd feared, he would pursue her. She'd been too young. Too vulnerable. But his excuses didn't matter.

He shouldn't have waited for her to ask. He should have *seen*. He should have been like Ilias and simply stepped in.

He was doing that now. And he wouldn't allow her pride get in his way.

CHAPTER SIX

RATHER THAN EAT dinner on the plane, Konstantin said they'd eat at the hotel, but it was already midnight, local time, when they landed.

"We're staying at Le Negresco?" Eloise blinked at the hundred-year-old icon of a building.

"Problem? I've never stayed in Nice, but my staff knows to get me the best," Konstantin said.

"They have. I've dined here with Mom. I doubt the kitchen will still be open, though."

"It's all arranged," Konstantin assured her.

It was. The concierge met them curbside with a bell-man who took their luggage. As they were escorted to their room, they were treated to a brief history of the building, which had been designed to bring artists and royalty to the French Riviera. It was filled with authentic period furniture and an abundance of fine art.

The concierge then showed them into a sea-view suite decorated in shades of rose pink and sage green. The bed had an ornate headboard of brass and quilted silk. Sheer drapes framed the doors to the balcony and a sitting area held mahogany furniture upholstered in striped silk. A welcome basket of fruit and chocolate sat on the coffee table. An ice bucket held a bottle of wine.

"Room service will be up shortly with the meal that your assistant requested," the concierge informed them with an obsequious smile.

"My room is through here?" Konstantin opened a door.

Eloise stepped forward to see through it, but it was only a bathroom.

They both looked for another door, but there was only the one from the hall, where the bellman was setting both of their bags.

"Pardon?" the concierge asked.

"*Où est l'autre chambre*?" Eloise tried in French.

"Ah." Understanding and apology flickered across the man's face. "There has been a misunderstanding. We were told two adults, not two rooms. At this time of year, we are fully booked. Tomorrow, perhaps, we could accommodate you in one of our larger suites. This is all we have for the moment."

"I thought this only happened to pregnant women on Christmas Eve," Eloise said out the side of her mouth.

Konstantin shot her a look of disbelief, then grimaced. "I didn't make clear to my assistant that I was no longer traveling with Gemma."

Lovely. He would have been perfectly happy to share a room with Ms. Tall, Blonde and Buxom, but not with her.

A quiet knock announced the arrival of the room service trolley.

"It's fine. We'll manage for tonight." Konstantin impatiently waved everyone from the room.

Once they were alone, he shrugged out of his jacket and threw it over the arm of the settee, letting out an exhale of frustration.

"It's late to call my mother, but I could try her?" Eloise offered.

"No. I don't want you going there alone. We managed to share a room last night without assault charges. I'm sure we can do it again tonight."

"I'll sleep on the sofa." Even though it was a relic with ornate wooden arms and—were these cushions actually stuffed with horsehair? She poked at one, thinking it had about as much give as a saddle.

"We can share the bed. You're so small I won't even notice you're there."

"Don't—" She clacked her teeth shut.

"Don't what?"

She crossed her arms, defensive, but always frustrated by this.

"I know I'm small, all right? People dismiss me as a child *all the time*. Mom does it." She waved her hand in exasperation. "Ilias was a big strong man so he was someone she could lean on, but I'm her little doll who she wants to dress up and gossip with and marry off so I'll have my own big strong man to protect me. I'm actually a grown-up, okay? I'd appreciate it if you'd treated me like one."

If he had been a panther, his tail would have twitched as he took in her outburst.

Her stomach knotted. She had an overwhelming sense that she'd made a horrible mistake in declaring herself an adult.

"I don't see you as a child, Eloise," he said in a quiet growl that nearly knocked her over. "I haven't for a long time."

Her heart seemed to fall right out of her body and the floor shifted beneath her. She didn't know what to do with that information. She grew so hot, so self-aware, it was painful. The room seemed to shrink and the air thinned so she couldn't draw enough of it into her lungs.

"Shall we eat?" He lifted the lid off a plate and the aroma of savory crepes under a drizzle of Dijon sauce wafted toward her.

Shakily, she joined him at the table, but it was so tiny their knees brushed when she tried to cross her legs.

"I...um... I think I'll run a bath after dinner, if that's okay? I slept so much on the flight I'm not tired yet." And she *really* needed some distance from him, even if it was only into the bathroom.

"You were really just overtired? I can book you to see a doctor if it's more serious."

"Are you still accusing me of using drugs? If I was into them, I'd take something to help me sleep, wouldn't I? No, I barely touch alcohol since someone spiked my drink." She waved at the wine she'd only sipped. "Drugs are the last thing I'd put in my body voluntarily."

"Who did that to you?" His ability to go from bored to deadly was really something. "What happened?"

"Nothing. Thankfully." She shrank into herself, though, still bothered by the incident. "I was at a house party. Not even a wild one. I thought I knew everyone there, so I wasn't vigilant about watching my glass. All of a sudden, I felt really dopey and sluggish. My girlfriend realized I'd been dosed and helped me get home."

"When was this?"

"After Ilias, when I was trying to at least pretend I was getting on with my life. But that's another reason I wanted a fresh start in New York. I didn't trust any of the people I thought I could."

"You do need a man to look after you," he muttered, stabbing his fork into his meal.

"You need to bite me," she muttered back.

His brows shot up. "Do you want to repeat that?"

"I may not be living my life to your standards, but I've been keeping myself alive."

"Barely."

"Losing Ilias was *hard*, Konstantin. Maybe not for you, but it was for me." She hung onto her composure, but her eyes grew hot and her throat tightened.

She poked and poked at her food, but couldn't bring any to her mouth.

"It was hard. Is." His admission was so quiet she almost didn't hear it, but the words seemed to catch at her heart and draw it out of her chest, pulling it out of shape in the process.

She wanted to reach out to him, to hang onto this small link they shared, even though that grief was so acidic it hurt to touch.

"Would you—?" She sipped to clear her throat. "I know you don't like to talk about yourself, but would you tell me a memory you have of him? Something I wouldn't know?" she asked tentatively.

His brows flinched together. He attacked his plate a moment, stabbing like he needed to kill it before he could eat it. "I'm not nostalgic, Eloise. I don't look back unless I have to."

She nodded mutely. "Okay," she murmured, even though his refusal made her ache with disappointment.

The silence between them grew weighted. The sound of their cutlery was overloud in the small room.

Then he spoke abruptly, sounding aggrieved that she had demanded this of him.

"I was far behind all my classmates when I arrived at boarding school. I didn't speak English. He was the only boy I could talk to."

She lifted her gaze in surprise and found his dark eyes

roiling with contained emotions that stalled her glass half-way to her mouth. She felt picked up and thrown around by those turbulent emotions. She slowly finished her sip, dampening her mouth with the cool tang of the wine, saying nothing so he could continue if he was willing to.

"Ilias was always in the top three while my grades were dead last. He tutored me for years." He jabbed at his food again. "He's the only reason I didn't flunk out within weeks of arriving. It was like that for years. Then one day in year nine, I earned a higher mark than his. It wasn't even top of the class, just one point higher than his. The culture was very competitive. Another boy would have accused me of cheating, but Ilias shook my hand and congratulated me. He was so happy for me it was embarrassing."

"Oh." She couldn't help her happy-sad chuckle, able to see her brother so clearly in that split second. He would have been grinning widely, admiring the paper, throwing his arm around his friend, building him up.

Her eyes welled and her chest ballooned with acute emotion. She sniffed.

"Don't *cry*." Konstantin's eyes widened in alarm. "I thought you would like it. You *asked* me to tell you that."

"I do like it. But I miss him so much sometimes." Her voice cracked. "And I can't talk to Mom about him because—that's another reason I haven't tried to see her. And why I didn't mind at first when Antoine was there. It's so stressful when we're together. We both want Ilias to be there, but he's not. And when we talk about h-him—" Her breaths grew jagged as she tried to push words around the sobs that were elbowing the inside of her rib cage, fighting to be released. "It's such a raw nerve, even after all this time." She used her napkin to wipe at her cheeks, but the tears kept rolling down them.

"Stop. Eloise, stop." He rose to drag her into his arms. "*I'll* be there," he said gruffly, practically smothering her face against his chest as he squeezed her in his strong arms. "It will be fine. Stop crying."

This embrace was what she had wanted from him for so long that her tears sharpened. Her stomach cramped with her effort to hold back, but she was shuddering with pent-up anxiety and despair.

"Shush," he insisted as he petted her hair. "It's going to be okay, Eloise. I'm going to make it okay. *Please* stop crying."

How was she supposed to stop when he was being so *nice*?

She gave in to impulse and wrapped her arms around his waist, clinging while trying, really trying, to stem the flow, but she was shaking and…

Wait. Was he also shaking?

She was so surprised she tilted her head back to see he was about to drop a kiss on her hair.

They both froze for several pulse beats. It was the garden after the funeral all over again. Their noses were almost touching, their lips an inch from meeting.

He drew in a sharp breath and his hand slid down her back, ironing her into him while making every cell in her body come alive.

Her toes pushed into the floor on instinct. She arched, feeling him hardening against her abdomen. As tingles of excitement raced through her blood, she offered her mouth, gaze on his parted lips, wanting—

He jerked his head up and set her back a step, exactly as he had those other times.

"Go have your bath," he said grittily. He picked up his wine and stepped onto the balcony, allowing a damp December wind to gust in.

* * *

What the hell was wrong with him? Pressing a weeping woman to his growing erection was just wrong.

He'd pushed her away and was letting the fine mist off the Mediterranean cool his ardor, but it wasn't doing a very good job. He could still feel the press of her modest breast and the curve of her lower back. He could smell her hair and—most erotic of all—had seen the way she reacted to him.

It had all percolated a rush of arousal into his groin and he shouldn't have even touched her. He wouldn't have, if she hadn't started crying. He didn't even know why he'd shared that corny memory. Absolutely everything about the past turned like knives inside him, but she had looked so entreating when she asked him to share something about Ilias. He had wanted her to know why her brother had meant so much to him and that he missed Ilias, too.

Maybe he had even thought talking about her brother would defuse the sexual tension between them and remind him why he needed to act honorably with Eloise.

He was doing a stellar job at that, wasn't he?

She had started to cry, though. He couldn't *bear* a woman's tears. It put him into a fight-or-flight response from childhood, when he had heard his mother crying. He'd felt so helpless then, trying to console her, listening to her promise she would find them a way to escape, to be safe.

It had ended in despair for both of them, every time.

Thankfully, as an adult, he rarely heard a woman cry. Once he'd come across an employee in a stairwell and once a lover had lost her dog. He'd distracted the first with a year of paid leave and the other with a generous donation to an animal rescue center.

Eloise was different. Her sorrow had gone straight under

his skin, stirring up his own grief, layers and layers of it. It was disturbing enough that his first thought was to fire up his jet and head to the Maldives.

But he couldn't. He'd not only promised her that he would be with her tomorrow, but he was still furious she was living, as she called it, so far below his standards. He took it as a personal failure on his part.

He should have been looking out for her all this time. When he thought of the number of men who had tried to take advantage of her, he could hardly contain his fury. And the idea of her holing up in a dorm room, unable to get herself to class, ground like a heel against his conscience. Of course, she would have been too devastated to get on with life. He should have *known* that. He should have done something far sooner than this.

He shouldn't have left it until she was living his worst nightmare: struggling and going hungry, unable to think of the future because today was so uncertain.

She *did* need someone looking out for her.

At the same time, he understood why she would rather struggle on her own terms than be beholden to a man like Antoine. If Konstantin had been older when his grandfather had come into his life, he might have rejected him and made his own way, too. He'd resented needing to rely on the old man, especially because his grandfather's "generosity" had come with its own costs and obligations.

He didn't want Eloise to think she owed him anything for his help so he had resisted the urge to crush her mouth with his, even though the plump, soft pout of her lips had been nearly irresistible.

When his grip on the iron rail of the balcony began radiating ice up his forearms, he stepped back inside the room. He was immediately assaulted by the fragrance of whatever beads she'd poured into the tub. As he topped up his glass of wine, the water shut off. He heard the ripple of water and the squeak of her naked body against the porcelain.

His lizard brain exploded with the image of her nude form all shiny and soapy, eyelids heavy with relaxation, mouth curved into a smile of invita—

No.

He yanked the leash on his libido.

She's Ilias's little sister. She's vulnerable.

She trusted him. And he'd already lied to her. He'd told her he wouldn't notice she was in the bed beside him, but he doubted he would sleep a wink.

CHAPTER SEVEN

ELOISE WAITED IN the bed while Konstantin brushed his teeth, telling herself this was no different than sharing the flat with her roommate where she took the sofa and her roommate had the murphy bed that came down from the wall.

This was very different, though.

This is what marriage would be like.

Routine intimacy. A shared bed during the most vulnerable time: sleep.

Going to bed together after a fight.

Not that they'd fought. No, it was worse than that. She had thrown herself at him and he'd turned her down *again*. They'd spoken in stilted tones after her bath, agreeing they should get some sleep. She'd waited until he was in the bathroom to take off the robe and put on her T-shirt and underwear to sleep in, then she'd climbed into bed and was trying to fall asleep by sheer willpower, hoping to be unconscious by the time he joined her.

The door opened and the light went off. Konstantin found his way to the bed. She didn't know what he was wearing. Behind her, the covers lifted and the mattress dipped. The blankets settled and he exhaled.

She stared blindly at the paisley pattern she couldn't really see in the wallpaper, trying not to move, but how was she supposed to sleep? She used to think about sharing a bed with him *all the time*. Sharing her *body*.

What diabolical biology made her obsess over him this way? She'd had plenty of offers from men over the years, but the kisses she'd invited had been pleasant rather than moving, the caresses more ticklish than erotic. No one had ever made her react the way she did to Konstantin, even though all she had with him were fantasies. She didn't even know *how* to make love. She'd never done it outside her imagination and that had always been with the man in this bed.

She tried not to let her mind wander down those avenues, tried not to move, even though she wanted to look at the clock. She distracted herself with trying to predict what would happen tomorrow. She berated herself for not making more of an effort when she'd first gone back to university, then spent some time listing all the solves for the world's current events. Nothing made her less aware of the man beside her.

Was he asleep? Or awake like her?

She couldn't sleep. She felt ripe. She felt as though her skin were thin and sensitized, her blood flowing fast beneath it. Her erogenous zones pulsed a signal of yearning, calling out to him, inviting his touch.

Then, miraculously, his hand was between her thighs, both soothing and inciting. His hot body surrounded hers; his lips caressed her nape. He said something against her ear that she didn't catch. She was too enthralled with the way he was sliding his touch between her folds. She was soaked and throbbing with arousal. His finger slid and teased and drew her closer and closer to climax, making her moan.

"Eloise."

She snapped awake to the silver light of early morning. Konstantin loomed over her, propped on his elbow. His hand on her shoulder flattened her to the mattress.

"Are you having a nightmare?"

"No." Her voice was throaty with the lust still gripping her.

He was close enough that she saw the way his pupils exploded, swallowing up the dark chocolate of his irises with inky black. His nostrils twitched and his gaze dropped to her mouth.

She reacted purely on instinct, not sure if it was dream or reality, but she rolled her hips toward him, reaching across to find his waist—his naked rib cage and the indent of his spine, inviting him closer.

With a noise that was half agony, half aggression, he dropped his head. His mouth capturing hers the way it had in Athens so long ago, with such ferocity she should have been alarmed, but she only curved closer while his hand swept behind her, drawing her even more fully under him.

If this was a continuation of the dream, she didn't care. The feel of him was glorious. His smooth back was beneath her splayed hand. His heavy chest crushed her aching breasts. His tongue sought her own, spearing excitement through her.

When his naked leg brushed hers, she moaned in supreme pleasure and luxuriated in the feel of his leg hair against the inside of her thigh and calf. He reacted by pushing his knee with more purpose between hers, pressing the ironlike tension of his thigh firmly against her mound.

Stars of sensation shot through her. She clamped her thighs on his, rocking her hips to increase the pressure, arching and rubbing, thrilling when his hand ran to her bottom and clenched into her cheek, possessive and encouraging her to keep rolling and writhing—

Climax struck. It wouldn't have happened if she hadn't already been halfway there in her dream, but here she was, thrust into the explosive joy of orgasm. She might have scratched his back. She definitely moaned long and loudly into his mouth.

His whole body went taut. For long seconds, he held her in place, letting the waves of orgasm wash over her.

When it began to subside, he slowly, almost tenderly, lifted his mouth from her panting lips. He brushed a strand of hair off her eyelashes and asked in a lust-soaked voice, "Are you even awake?"

Reality crashed over her with such mortification she groaned, "No. I mean, yes, but—"

He was already leaving the bed, swearing as he threw back the covers and locked himself in the bathroom with a firm click of the door. The shower came on.

She rolled her face into the pillow and kicked her feet against the mattress, wishing she could run to the other side of the world.

Eloise was going to be the death of him, she really was.

Konstantin came out of a shower where he'd had to—*had to*—take himself in hand and relieve the urgency gripping him.

He found the room empty. *Damn it.* He knew he shouldn't have touched her. Even as he had kissed her, a voice in his head had been bellowing that he should stop.

That kiss, though. He'd waited six long years to taste her again, telling himself he'd imagined how incredible she was, but that had been every bit as potent as he recalled. As he'd feared. She'd rolled into him and slid her leg along his and those signals of receptiveness had short-circuited his brain. There'd been no thought in his head except to plunder the mouth that was opening to him. To drag her closer and feel more of her.

When his thigh had notched against the cotton of her underwear, the heat of her had scorched his thigh, hardening him to acute anticipation. He had palmed her pert ass while she rolled her hips and then she had just *dissolved*.

It had been exquisite and exciting as hell, but that's also when he realized she might not be fully aware she was in bed with him.

That thought was enough of a slap to regain control of himself, if not a cold enough shock to fully douse his arousal.

Who the hell had she been dreaming of, though?

The question grated in him as he hurried to dress, only realizing as he was pocketing his phone that there was a blurred shape standing on the balcony.

He yanked open the door. "What are you doing out here?"

"Questioning my life choices." She had her coat collar turned up around her chin. Her eyes were big enough to swallow her face. "What are you doing?"

"Going down for breakfast. Do you want to come?" The moment the words emerged from his mouth, he heard the double entendre.

So had she. A fierce blush bloomed across her face.

He turned back into the room, leaving the door open for her. Normally, he dined in the privacy of his room, but they needed space and other people and the grating whine of a child who'd risen too early.

Otherwise, they would finish wrecking that damned bed.

* * *

Eloise didn't want to talk about it, but had the impending sense that they should. Not that she was willing to bring it up in a busy dining room. All she managed to say was that her mother would serve at least three courses at lunch so they should eat lightly.

Konstantin nodded a curt acknowledgment, then ordered pastries and coffee for them. She kept her eyes on a French newspaper she stole off a nearby table. Konstantin exchanged messages with someone in a battery of muted buzzes from his phone.

This was excruciating. While she pretended to read, she was hyperaware of him. Her body was alternating between the heat of embarrassment and the heat of arousal. She couldn't glance at his mouth without remembering how ravenous his kiss had been. Any small shift of his body reminded her of the imposing weight of him against her. When he absently cupped his coffee, she remembered the feel of his palm branding her bottom.

He'd been hard against her thigh, his heart slamming so hard she'd felt it against her breast. She'd been feeling sexy and desired and buttery with her receding climax when he'd asked her if she was awake.

Now he was Mr. Remote again, barely speaking to her.

"Do you need anything from the room?" he asked as they were finishing their second coffee. "My car is waiting."

"We can't go to Mom's yet. She'll still be in bed."

"You need something to wear." His tone was somewhere between patient and patronizing.

She looked down at the clothes he'd bought her in New York. They were a fast-fashion solution to an immediate problem and the few things she'd brought from the apartment were even more wrinkled and tired. She didn't want to go further into his debt, but knew he was right. She couldn't turn up like this.

"I just need my coat," she murmured.

A short time later, Konstantin walked her into a busy salon where a stylist introduced herself as Ghaliya.

"I thought I was picking out a dress, not having a full makeover," Eloise grumbled as she saw a nail tech preparing her station for her.

"You said you didn't want Antoine to know how much you've struggled," he pointed out dispassionately, eyes on the wall of nail polish arranged in bands like a rainbow.

"What sort of look are we going for today?" Ghaliya asked brightly as she returned from hanging Eloise's coat. "Are you attending a holiday event? A special occasion perhaps?"

"Return of a prodigal daughter?" Eloise asked with a facetious quirk of her mouth in Konstantin's direction. He might as well have some say, since he was paying for it.

"This isn't an apology tour. It's a triumphant return," he stated firmly, then frowned. "Are you going to cut your hair?"

She shot a protective hand to the ponytail at her nape. "A trim, maybe. Why? Should I?" She'd worn it short through her teens and early twenties, only letting it grow out lately because she hadn't had the will or funds to cut it. She had rediscovered she liked having long hair.

"With your features, a pixie or a bob would be very cute," Ghaliya said with enthusiasm.

"*No*," Konstantin said in firm refusal.

Eloise drew her brows in question, puzzled by his emphatic reaction.

"That length suits you," he stated, cheek ticking even as he looked away. "But do whatever you want."

"I used to wear it short, but I prefer it long." Eloise played her fingers against her nape, not sure what to make of his opinion.

"It sounds like you know what you want," Ghaliya said diplomatically. "Shall we get started? Did you want to make yourself comfortable, sir? We should be finished by eleven if you'd rather come back. We'll be across the street at the boutique by then."

"I'll meet you there." Konstantin held Eloise's gaze as though he was waiting for her to confirm she would be okay if he left.

She nodded jerkily, kind of touched that he was so considerate, but also worried by how dependent she was becoming on him. Maybe she had more of her mother's tendencies than she'd ever realized, because the minute he left, she felt abandoned.

On the other hand, given all that had happened since the elevator doors had opened in that New York high-rise two days ago, she desperately needed time and space away from him to process.

Ghaliya didn't give her a chance to dwell on any of that, though. She distracted her with a thousand small decisions around hair, nails and makeup while keeping up a pleasant chatter of innocuous topics like celebrity gossip and the latest fashions.

Before Eloise knew it, she was in the boutique across the street, staring at someone who was both recognizable and a complete stranger.

Her hair had been highlighted and trimmed to create a gold frame around her face and generous waves had been pressed into it, making it look shiny and casually polished.

The longer length and shape did suit her. Those old pixie cuts had made her eyes seem too big for her face, but with a subtle touch of makeup and an understated lipstick, the balance was just right.

For clothes, she chose a cashmere sweater in fern green over a wrap skirt with diagonal buttons on her hip. It left a good portion of her left leg bare, revealing her black tights and tall boots. She was trying a beret when Konstantin entered.

His imposing presence immediately soaked up all the oxygen in the exclusive shop, making the walls shrink in around her.

In an effort to move past all the awkwardness of this morning, Eloise turned and dropped her hand on her hip, throwing her weight to one side while pointing with her other hand at the hat. "Chic? Or overkill?"

The way his inscrutable gaze traveled all over her made her feel as exposed as a doe in a field, sending a small zing through her that urged her to run.

"Keep it," he said in a deep voice. "It's cold out."

Practical, she noted with a twinge of letdown.

"Let me get you some jacket options," the stylist murmured as she disappeared to another section of the small store.

Eloise turned back to the mirror and fiddled with the hat, surreptitiously glancing at Konstantin in the reflection, wondering if he was still cross with her over the way she'd behaved when they'd woken.

His gaze was caressing her butt!

A tingling sensation of his hand there had been torturing her all morning. Now a fresh rush of heat flooded into her loins as she remembered the satisfying sensation of his hard thigh pressing against the tender, throbbing flesh, tipping her into a place so delicious her mouth dried as she remembered it.

His gaze came up to meet hers in the mirror and she couldn't make herself look away, even though she was accosted by the memory of moaning into his mouth, holding onto him as her body quaked.

Making it worse, he knew exactly what was in her mind.

"Who were you dreaming about?" he asked in a voice that sounded as though it originated in the bottom of his chest.

She flinched and was finally able to drop her gaze. "I don't want to say."

"Why not? I won't be angry."

Did he really imagine it could be anyone but him? She rolled her lips together, deeply culpable as she lifted a painful glance that was so revealing it made her cheeks and throat hurt.

She heard his sharp inhale, then Ghaliya bustled back.

"This one or...? Oh. *Je m'excuse.* I'll leave you two alone," she murmured and turned away, trying to escape whatever charged air was between them.

"No. We're expected for lunch," Konstantin said. "Has my assistant given you everything you need?"

"*Oui. Merci.*" Ghaliya gave him a warm smile of appreciation. "And Mademoiselle Eloise has my card if she needs anything else. This one would be better, I think," she added to Eloise, offering the shorter jacket.

Konstantin took it to hold it for her, making her feel clumsy as she threaded her arms into the sleeves.

She waited until they were in the car to say, "Thank you for all of this." She waved from hair to shoes. She was genuinely grateful, feeling more confident and less like a petitioner begging for handouts. "Will you please send me the invoice? I know I'm a long way from paying you back, but—"

"And risk breaking your phone?" Konstantin drawled. He plucked something from the console between them and offered it. "This is for you, by the way."

It was a new phone, one that was already activated. It was even in a pretty brushed gold case that had a designer's initials etched into it.

"*Please* don't put me this far into your debt," she bemoaned, tucking her fists into her lap rather than accept it.

"You're being ridiculous. My number is in there. I expect you to use it whenever you need something." He dropped the device into her lap.

She caught it so it wouldn't slip to the floor, then found his number along with a second one for someone named *Nemo*, whoever that was. She texted Konstantin.

Please send me a copy of the invoice.

His phone dinged and he glanced at it, sighed, then sent her a flat look. "I only argue about things that matter, Eloise. This topic is closed."

"I'll ask Ghaliya, then." She opened the faux snakeskin clutch to search out the stylist's card.

"It's a *gift*. What was that twelve days of nonsense you were doing? Consider it that." He flicked his hand as though it were inconsequential.

"Goody. Seven more days of this?" She pressed her hands to her sandwiched phone and smiled with sarcastic excitement.

"Yes. Now I don't want to hear another word about it."

Oh, this man. She bit back arguing further, though. The car was turning into the gates of her mother's villa and the butterflies in her stomach became a swarm of bees that moved into her chest. She dropped the phone into her clutch and rubbed her damp palm onto her skirt.

Konstantin's hand came across to capture hers. He frowned at how cold her fingers were.

"It will be fine. I promise."

She wanted to believe him so she nodded as though she did.

CHAPTER EIGHT

ACCORDING TO THE reports Konstantin had received from his assistant, Ilias's mother had stayed in Athens for the first year after Ilias died. Then she had begun traveling with friends, dating a number of men before attaching herself to Antoine. They had dated, became engaged, then moved to Nice once they married. They'd been here three years.

Her new husband had money, yes, but none of it had been earned through any serious effort on his part. He had inherited a modest fortune at eighteen from an aunt. He then married one of his aunt's friends, an older woman with a heart condition. She had passed within a few years, leaving Antoine a tidy sum that allowed him to penetrate higher social circles. The next time he married, it was a French pop star. She divorced him fairly quickly, granting him a shockingly large settlement on his way out the door. That suggested to Konstantin that she'd done whatever necessary to get him out of her life.

After that, he'd had a string of long-term relationships with wealthy women of an appropriate age, all well-placed in Europe's highest social circles. He was the sort of man who thought he should have been born an aristocrat and would have been the worst kind if he had.

Konstantin had asked his assistant to track down the retired trustee, Cyrus, but discreetly, so it was taking time.

The car stopped in front of a quiet fountain. A butler hurried out with an umbrella, even though the rain was barely spitting.

Konstantin came around and took it, tempted to set his hand in Eloise's lower back, but he couldn't trust himself to keep his touch bolstering rather than a caress of appreciation. He was determined to be her bodyguard right now. Her wingman. Nothing more.

But he'd always found her naturally attractive with her eyes looking green in some light and gold in others. Her features had lovely symmetry and the corners of her mouth tilted upward in an appealing way, even when she was somber, as she was now.

When he'd entered the shop a short while ago, he'd been spellbound by her. Her mood had been light, her pose cheeky. She'd been carefree and so beautiful he'd instantly been awash in want.

God did he want her. He'd spent the hours apart from her trying not to think of the way she'd reached for him this morning, only to shudder with orgasm. He'd barely touched her! It was the most erotic thing he'd ever experienced and he damned well wanted more. He'd been fighting that craving, but as they'd stood in the shop, he hadn't been able to resist asking whom she had been dreaming of.

Her look of guilt had punched straight into his groin. He'd nearly shouted to clear the store so he could take her right then and there. His desire for her had been so obvious the stylist had recognized it in an instant and tried to excuse herself.

Pay attention, he ordered himself as they entered a foyer

where a curved staircase swept to the upper floor and a domed ceiling held a sparkling chandelier.

"Eloise!" Lilja rushed toward them from a door to their left. She barely glanced at him, too anxious to embrace her daughter.

Lilja was a little taller than Eloise, but not much. Her blond hair had turned to silver since Konstantin had seen her last, but otherwise she was the same classic beauty she had always been. She was slender and elegant and closed her eyes as she held onto Eloise and drew in a savoring breath.

"I've *missed* you."

"I've missed you, too, Mom. But—" Eloise rubbed her mother's back "—did you see who I brought with me?"

"Hmm? Oh, I presumed this was your driver. *Konstantin*!" Lilja laughed into her hand. "I'm so sorry. Goodness, look at you!" She set her light hands on his arms and offered her cheeks for his kiss.

"I've been called worse," he said with genuine amusement. "How are you, Lilja? When Eloise told me she was seeing you, I insisted on coming along."

"I'm so glad," she said with misty sincerity, but sent a disconcerted look toward the door she'd come through. "You'll stay for lunch, of course. Tell the kitchen we're five, please, Marcel," she said to the hovering butler before looping her arm through both of theirs. "Come say hello. Have you met my husband, Konstantin? I don't think so."

Her smile seemed forced as she escorted them into a high-ceilinged parlor where the view beyond the windows looked to the horizon of the Med.

A pair of men rose from their armchairs. One was white-haired and slightly paunchy beneath his bespoke suit. The other was closer to Konstantin's age, clean-shaven and might be called boyishly handsome. He struck Konstantin as cocksure in his trendy plaid trousers, his thick cardigan pushed up to his elbows and his button shirt open at his throat.

Both men eyed him with keen yet somewhat hostile interest.

"Antoine, you'll never guess who Eloise has brought with her today."

"I'm sure I won't since I didn't expect her to bring anyone." There was a subtle edge to Antoine's tone that Konstantin immediately disliked.

"It's nice to see you," Eloise said weakly, stepping away from Lilja and moving so her stepfather could kiss her cheeks. "This is Konstantin Galanis. He was one of Ilias's closest friends. I'm sure Mom must have mentioned him."

She stepped aside so Konstantin could shake Antoine's hand. They took each other's measure with one succinct pump.

"Edoardo Ricci is also a good friend of the family," Lilja said.

The other man stepped forward. "It's so good to see you again, Eloise." Edoardo's hands came up as though to take hold of Eloise's upper arms.

Her recoil was only slight, but Konstantin reacted reflexively. He locked his arm across her back and splayed possessive fingers on her hip, tucking her into his side.

Edoardo's expression blanked. He dropped his hands and offered Konstantin a limp shake with a weak, "*Kýrie* Galanis. I'm familiar with your name and organization. It's a pleasure to meet you."

Konstantin nodded, always willing to let silence do his talking.

For a stalled moment, there was only the crackle of the

fire in the fireplace and the imagined crackle of animosity coming off Antoine toward him.

"Sit. Tell us how you came to deliver Eloise to us today," Antoine invited, then waved his empty glass at the butler. "More cognac. Mimosas for the girls."

Konstantin waited while Eloise sat on the sofa before he lowered beside her. He hitched his pant leg as he crossed his legs and extended his arm along the back of the sofa behind her, angling himself more to Lilja than his host. Deliberately.

"Are you feeling as well as you look, Lilja?" Konstantin asked.

"I am," Lilja assured him with a fluttering smile of pleasure. "Oh, thank you, Marcel."

The atmosphere grew charged again as the butler set out the fresh drinks. Edoardo's confusion was a blinking neon light while Konstantin could feel Antoine staring holes into the side of his head.

As the butler left them alone, Lilja asked, "Am I to understand… Are you two seeing each other? Has this been going on long?"

"No." Konstantin sensed Eloise stiffening beside him and reached for her hand, signaling that she should let him do the talking.

She rose and moved across the room. "Your tree looks pretty, Mom."

Trying to shift the conversation?

"I wasn't sure about the silver and blue," Lilja said reflectively, twisting slightly to continue speaking to her. "I may ask the decorator to change it to something more traditional before our party tomorrow night. You'll come, won't you?" She directed that to Konstantin. "It's nothing fancy, just a festive little soiree for whoever is in town."

"We'd love to." Konstantin took far too much pleasure in goading the other men by claiming Eloise as his date.

How Eloise felt about it was a mystery. She was trailing her hands along the polished maple of the grand piano before she lightly touched a few keys.

"Are you going to play for us, darling?" Lilja asked with coaxing warmth. "That would be nice. It's been too long."

"Marcel is looking for us to go into the dining room," Antoine said.

Konstantin turned his head to stare the man down. He had already decided he hated him before he met him, but as Eloise sat and picked out a few notes, it occurred to him that this viper had deliberately kept her from something else she loved: music.

Eloise ignored Antoine and set her hands into unhurried chords that gradually arranged themselves into what Konstantin recognized as "I'll Be Home for Christmas."

He looked back to where she gracefully swayed to reach the keys, manifesting the gentle climb and fall of emotions in the song. Her eyes were closed, her profile glowing in the light off the tree.

Konstantin didn't know all the words, but he knew it was about homesickness and nostalgia. As yearning flowed from her hands to fill the room and vibrate in his chest, his throat ached.

The sadness might have swamped him completely, but she somehow layered in tentative hope as she reached the end.

She sang the final words very softly as she slowed the tempo even more, searching out the last chords with supreme care. A lifetime of wishes hovered in the silence before the final note ended the song.

Konstantin was utterly captivated. His body felt rusted

into place, his consciousness having been stolen and transported elsewhere.

"*Brava*, darling. That was beautiful," Lilja said as she wiped tears from her cheeks, but she was smiling widely. They were happy tears and they tugged differently in his chest, making him fiercely glad he'd given her this reunion with her daughter. "That was truly the best Christmas present I could ever have," she said to Konstantin. "Thank you."

"My pleasure," he said, meaning it.

Antoine stood and bent over Lilja so he broke their eye contact. He offered his wife a handkerchief and rubbed her shoulder.

"My sensitive little love. We were at the opera a few weeks ago and she cried her way through that, too. Didn't you? Shall we go to the table?"

They all stood and Eloise left the piano to join them.

"That was very good," Edoardo said.

"Parlor tricks," she claimed with a self-deprecating smile.

Hardly. Konstantin had never been moved by sleight of hand or the flair of a bartender. The fact he was feeling so unsettled by a dated Christmas carol was disturbing in the extreme. He much preferred numbness over this agonizing prickle that resembled a return of sensation to a limb that had fallen asleep. Typically, when something affected him, he removed himself the way he would back away from a bonfire that threatened to light his clothes on fire, but that option wasn't open to him right now, was it?

"You're the guest of honor. You can escort Lilja," Antoine said to Konstantin as though this were a royal procession. "I'll take Eloise." He crooked his arm imperiously.

Lilja gathered her composure and set her hand on Konstantin's arm.

"Actually, you go in with Edoardo. I need a word with Marcel," Antoine said, stepping back at the last second to wave the younger man toward Eloise.

Did the man think he was playing chess? And winning?

As they arrived into the dining room, and the butler transferred their drinks to the table, Konstantin saw how Antoine was continuing his puerile machinations. The seating arrangements were meant to put Edoardo between Eloise and her mother. Eloise was positioned at Antoine's left, while Konstantin was supposed to sit across from her and closer to her mother's end of the table.

As Konstantin seated Lilja, he ordered Edoardo, "Eloise can sit there. I'll sit next to her." He nodded at the chair closest to Lilja. Edoardo could visit Siberia on the other side of the table.

"Lilja prefers the proper etiquette of alternating ladies and gentleman," Antoine told him with a patronizing smile.

"The women want to catch up so we'll indulge them." Konstantin could play the doting game, too.

Antoine looked to Edoardo, perhaps seeking an ally, but Edoardo was canny enough to see he had a decision to make: whether to stick with whatever Antoine had promised him or curry favor with the much bigger fish that was Konstantin Galanis for the bank that bore his family name.

Edoardo took the chair on the far side of the table.

The meal went on forever. Konstantin participated in the expected topics of sports and politics and business, all the while listening to Eloise deflect her mother's probing inquiries about their relationship by asking after mutual acquaintances.

When Edoardo excused himself to make a call, and Lilja was busy relaying details of a play she'd seen recently, Antoine leaned toward Konstantin.

"What exactly is your intention here?" He flicked his gaze toward Eloise. "Is this a dalliance for your own entertainment? Because I have responsibilities where my wife's daughter is concerned. There are things I won't allow."

Konstantin was rarely taken aback by the levels that a man could sink to, but he was genuinely astonished that Antoine would accuse him of being a womanizer. And was casting himself as the guardian best suited to protect her. Exactly how desperate was he to marry her to Edoardo? *Why?*

The women stopped speaking, sensing the change in temperature.

Edoardo returned with a polite, "I apologize—" He cut himself off as he came up against the wall of hostility between the men.

Antoine held Konstantin's penetrating gaze and Konstantin wondered if the man was dangerously obtuse or simply too arrogant to see how far out of his league he was.

"A dalliance?" Konstantin repeated with disdain, abandoning good manners. "No. I don't use women for entertainment. I certainly wouldn't start with the sister of my best friend."

"I'm sure Antoine didn't mean to imply anything like that," Eloise murmured in a soothing undertone. Her hand found his arm, trying to stay his temper.

He flashed her a glare of outrage because he had heard what he heard.

Anxiety pinched her mouth and there was a line of tension across her cheekbones that seemed to repeat what she had asked him in New York.

What are you going to do? Shatter her beliefs and force her to suffer yet another heartbreak? She would blame me.

He shot his attention to Lilja. She was staring into her

plate, blinking back tears, seeming mortified that her luncheon had gone sour.

Look after your daughter, he wanted to shout at her. But hurting Lilja would hurt Eloise, and Lilja was not the villain here. Antoine was. Ilias would expect Konstantin to protect his family from such a man, but how?

The answer arrived the way intuition struck sometimes, when Konstantin saw the way forward long before he had worked through the logistics and reasoning behind it. If Konstantin were the fanciful type, he would say Ilias whispered the solution in his ear.

"My intention is to ask for your blessing, Lilja." Konstantin was far too pleased with the choked noise that came out of Antoine. "Eloise and I are marrying."

CHAPTER NINE

"KONSTANTIN," ELOISE BREATHED, APPALLED.

"We weren't planning to announce it today." Konstantin rose and drew Eloise onto her feet and into his arms.

"No, we weren't." Her limbs didn't feel connected to her body. She pressed weakly at his chest, but it took all her control to lock her knees rather than collapse in a heap.

"But look how happy this news makes your mother."

Oh, that was just evil, stopping her protests in her throat.

"Oh, darling," her mother said weepily, eyes bright with joy.

"Mom—" She hesitated to slap that look off her mother's face with the truth, but there was no way she could lie to her about something like this.

Konstantin's arms tightened around her, pressing tingles of sensual memory through her skin and muscle and blood cells, urging her to go along.

Was he drunk?

But even as she tried to find the words to say that Konstantin was full of it, his ruse got rid of one very sticky problem.

"As I was saying, I've been called away," Edoardo blurted. "Happy news. Congratulations." With one final wild look toward Antoine, Edoardo made his escape.

Ironically, Eloise wished she could go with him. The malice she felt coming off Antoine was so thick it oozed.

Antoine rose to shake Konstantin's hand in a very perfunctory way. "Congratulations."

"Thank you. Eloise was concerned you would be upset." Konstantin held Antoine's stare in challenge.

"Antoine has only ever wanted what's best for you, darling. I hope you know that." Her mother rose to embrace each of them, but Eloise felt Antoine's malignant glare. He was more than upset. He was blistering with such fury Eloise couldn't help pressing into Konstantin's solid presence when her mother stepped back.

"No ring yet?" Her mother kept her hand, and covered it with her own, exclaiming, "Darling! You can wear my ring from Petros. It's in the safe. No." She touched her chin as she started to turn away. "The box at the bank in Athens. We'll have to make a special trip," she said to Antoine.

"In the New Year, perhaps." Antoine manufactured a lovey-dovey smile. "We're expected in Como for Christmas. Remember? You're looking forward to seeing Melissa."

"That's true, but..." Her brows drew together in consternation.

"Mom, that's not necessary," Eloise protested.

This isn't even real.

"I want you to have it," her mother insisted. "It would have gone to Ilias for his wife and it bothers me that it's locked away. Ilias would want you to wear it, especially if you're marrying Konstantin." She tilted a watery smile up at him. "You're practically family already."

Did Konstantin flinch? If he did, he masked it before Eloise had registered more than a twitch of his arm around her and the bob of his Adam's apple as he swallowed.

"That's kind of you to say, Lilja."

"Shall we sit and finish our meal?" Antoine said tersely, attempting to take control by moving to hold Lilja's chair.

"And champagne, please, Marcel," her mother instructed as she sat. "Oh, there's so much to discuss. Have you set a date?"

"Nothing is decided yet," Eloise stressed.

Don't get attached, Mom.

Did Konstantin not understand how wrong it was to build her mother's expectations like this?

"Yes, there is much to discuss," Konstantin agreed as he held Eloise's chair. His tone was both pleasant and lethal. "Details of the prenup," he added in Antoine's direction. "I have interests to protect as well."

For once, Eloise allowed herself a huge gulp of alcohol when the champagne arrived.

"What—" she could barely keep the pitch of her voice to a level tone as the car left her mother's front steps "—the hell."

"It's the most expedient solution," Konstantin said in that same tone of finality that he'd used earlier when he'd said, *I only argue about things that matter.*

"It's a bluff and he knows it." She curled her cold fists, still shaking from Antoine's warning as they left. "He just said to me, *don't come in here with a gun that's not loaded.*"

Konstantin turned his head to give her a look that was unimpressed. "I can't decide if the man genuinely lacks intelligence or is so driven by desperation he's becoming reckless. Either way, he is the one holding the gun and he's already shot himself in the foot with it."

"How? You've made things so much worse." She propped

her elbow next to the window and covered her eyes. "You heard Mom. She's already planning the wedding."

"Good. Now you have a reason to speak to her as often as you like."

"What am I supposed to do? Let her think it's real for a year, then yank the rug? I told you I don't want to hurt her."

"Tempted as I am to force Antoine to foot the bill on an extravagant wedding that winds up canceled, we're not waiting a year." He glanced at his phone as it pinged, then touched the driver's shoulder.

"Sir?" The driver removed his ear bud.

"The jeweler has agreed to come to us. You can drop us at our hotel."

"Very good, sir." He screwed the bud back into his ear and made the turn to the Promenade des Anglais.

"What jeweler?" Eloise hissed.

"The one providing your ring. Wear anything your mother gives you if it makes you happy, but you'll wear my ring at that party tomorrow."

"For Antoine's sake? You're taking this too far," she protested. "I'm glad you put Edoardo on the run. Thank you for that. Really. But Antoine is not stupid. He knows I have nothing going for me beyond passable looks and presumed fertility. That's why he offered me to a man who wants a society wife and a vessel for his heir. He thinks it would put Edoardo in his debt. *You* don't have to settle for someone who is broke, though. Antoine knows that."

"Thank God you're here to explain patriarchy to me. I've never gotten the hang of it."

"No, you're doing it right," she assured him. "This game of chicken you've entered into with Antoine is a classic use of a woman to one-up another man. But I refuse to be part of it. This lie has gone far enough. I can't mess with my mother like that."

"Eloise." He frowned at her. "I'm not sure where the communication has broken down. Do you not realize I'm serious? We're marrying."

"What?" Her heart lurched. Maybe she was still asleep in her bed in New York and none of this had happened. She pinched her arm, half expecting to wake up on the subway, cold and hungry and miserable.

She was awake, though. This was real. Her blood was skimming so fast through her arteries her whole body vibrated. Her inner seventeen-year-old wanted to faint with excitement, but she was a sensible adult now. She knew dreams were only dreams. They never came true.

"We can divorce later," Konstantin added in a throwaway rumble. "If necessary."

And there it was. The wake-up call. He didn't really want her. Why would he? That was why Antoine wasn't taking this seriously. Her stepfather knew as well as anyone that she brought nothing to a marriage.

The car stopped at the curb and the bellman rushed to open her door, giving her the chance to mutter over her shoulder, "Romantic as your proposal is, I'd rather swim back to New York and pick up toys from the gutter."

Her exit would have been glorious if she didn't have to go back to the room they shared for her passport and other effects.

Konstantin caught up to her as she stepped into the elevator. His expression was an iron mask as he took her hand before she could touch the button for their floor. Her heart leaped, but he was only forestalling her so he could choose a different button.

"They've moved us to a bigger suite."

"I just want my things," she said stiffly, pulling her hand free and trying to put space between them in the close confines of the elevator.

When the doors opened, a starlet and her entourage were waiting, everyone gabbling gaily.

Eloise pressed a smile onto her lips and stepped out, still shaking with turbulent emotions.

Konstantin led her to a door that he unlocked before he leaned to push it open, allowing her to precede him into the room.

It was even more beautiful than the one they had shared last night. An abundance of windows offered bright views overlooking the sea. There was a sitting room and inside one of the bedrooms, a young woman was putting away clothes. Bags and bags of them.

"What—? *Konstantin.*"

"Oh! Shall I come back?" the startled young woman asked in French.

"*Oui. Merci.*" Eloise was barely hanging on to her fraying temper. As the maid left, she turned on him. "You're doing exactly what Antoine did. You're telling me what's going to happen and assuming I'll go along with it."

His head went back. "That's insulting."

"Am *I* not allowed to be insulted? You proposed marriage *out of spite.*" It was especially hurtful coming from him, the man she'd girlishly dreamed of marrying. "You slapped him in the face with me as the gauntlet. Excuse me while I don't fawn all over you for treating me like chattel. I'm not a tool or a weapon. I'm not—"

Oh, she was going to cry. This was so humiliating.

Locking her throat against the bubble of pressure trying to burst free, she moved into the bedroom and searched for her long coat, double-checking that her passport was still in its zipped inner pocket. It was, along with her well-worn and mostly empty wallet. She took off the jacket she was wearing, throwing it onto the bed.

"Think this through, Eloise," Konstantin said crisply. "Negotiating the prenup forces Antoine to open your mother's financial books to me. If there's malfeasance, I'll find it and put a stop to it. You want that."

She did, but—

"He can't marry you to anyone else if you're married to me, can he?"

No, but… "I don't have to marry anyone if I don't want to," she blurted, still hurt by his drive-by proposal. "Especially when it's only a ridiculous stunt. You really want to go through all of this trouble and expense, buy me clothes and a ring, stage a *wedding* and negotiate a prenup just so you can get a peek inside a few ledgers? Fake a business deal with him," she cried, waving her hand in the air. "There are thousands of ways you could sic accountants on him."

"How are you missing that marriage accomplishes so much more than that?" He clasped the top of the door where he stood. "Think of the power and influence you'll have. He thought you'd make a good society wife? Hell, yes, you will. If you are my wife, no one will dare cross you, least of all him. And if he were to somehow steal all of your mother's money—which I won't allow to happen, but if he did—you'd have the means to support her."

"How?" she cried. "You *just* said we'd divorce."

"*If* necessary," he repeated.

"How could it not be necessary? You don't *want* to marry me."

"Of course, I want to. I don't do things I don't want to do," he said pithily.

"Yes, I know that," she said heatedly. "You've pushed me away enough times to make that very obvious." She hated to bring that up. It made her stomach hurt, the rejections were so sharp, but it was the truth.

"Really?" He dropped his arm to his side. "You're upset that I didn't kiss you when you were seventeen? *You were seventeen.*"

"What about the funeral?"

"It was a *funeral*. And last night you were crying."

"I wasn't crying this morning, was I? But you still couldn't get out of bed fast enough!"

His brows shot up. After a pause that caused her heart to batter the inside of her chest like a trapped bird, he said in a low rasp, "If I'd stayed in that bed, we would be marrying anyway because I didn't have a condom. I do now, by the way."

Gulp. She tried to look away, but the man was the king of staring contests, able to put erotic visions in her head with eye contact alone and forcing her to hold that vision between them until her scalp tightened. So did her nipples.

"We don't have to marry to have sex," she mumbled, hugging herself. Then she put up a hand, even though he hadn't moved. "That wasn't an invitation. I'm just saying that insisting on marriage is an overreaction."

"No, Eloise." His voice hardened. "What I've done until now has been an *under*-reaction." He pushed off the door so he filled the whole space with his powerful presence. "I cannot believe I left you and your mother to your own devices for this long. Marrying you is a correction. A necessary one. I intend to provide for your needs for the rest of your life. I intend to look out for your mother to the best of my ability. Marriage is the most expedient way to do those things."

"And what do you get out of it? A clean conscience? Sex?"

"Yes."

"You know that's not any more romantic than marrying me out of spite, right?"

He muttered a tired curse toward the ceiling.

"Look." She hugged the coat she still held. "I'm tempted to let you take over and look after us. That's a really nice offer, but as far as making corrections goes, I want to be strong enough to help my mother myself. Using you to do it makes me feel like I'm not enough. Like I'm still a—" She cut herself off and looked at her coat, wondering what she thought she was doing. Where would she go if she walked out? To her mother and Antoine?

"Still a what?" he prompted gruffly.

She threw the coat on the bed and took a few restless paces between the bed and the open wardrobe.

"Mom never *called* me a burden. She never said she didn't want me, but she didn't intend to have me. She met my father while she was on vacation. They had a brief affair and she didn't realize she was pregnant until it was too late to make other choices. And it was all on her to raise me. Dad was never there to change a diaper or anything."

"Did *she* change a diaper?" His brow went up with skepticism.

"No. I had nannies, obviously. But paying for them came out of the fortune that Ilias's father left her. My father didn't give her anything but a responsibility she hadn't asked for."

"Has she ever said anything to make you think she regrets having you?" he asked with gentle challenge.

"Not in a mean way. More like mother–daughter advice. Like, she was always very frank telling me about sex and warning me that pregnancy and babies are harder than anyone tells you. And that once you have a baby with someone, you're connected for life so, you know, choose wisely. It was a warning not to get into her situation."

"Your father was never part of your life at all?"

"I saw him a few times a year, but I was really young. My only strong memory is a yelling match when I was five or so. Ilias was thirteen so I asked him about it years later. Dad had tried to talk Mom into letting me go on the circuit with him, but she was afraid he would forget me somewhere or I'd drown. It's kind of heartening to know he wanted more of a relationship with me, but then he died and…" She shrugged. "It really was on Mom to support me. With Ilias's money."

"Ilias would never have begrudged his inheritance going to your upbringing. It was her money when you were a child and it is again. I think you're letting Antoine's manipulations get into your head."

"But he's not *wrong.* You're right that Ilias made it seem natural that Drakos money would pay for my upkeep. I took for granted that it always would, until Antoine called me a freeloader."

"He is *not* one to talk."

"But he has a point. It's time that I looked after Mom, not the other way around."

"You can't. I'm not saying that to be cruel. It's the truth."

She bit her lip, angered by reality, but unable to refute it.

"I understand where you're coming from, Eloise. I *hated* that I needed Ilias's help. I couldn't have saved my grandfather's company without him and your allowing me to help you allows me to let go of my own sense of having fallen short."

"But you *shouldn't* feel that way," she insisted, taking a few steps toward him. "If Ilias was in this predicament, then fine. You could marry him. But—"

"Don't make jokes," he said sharply. "Ilias is one of the few people I ever trusted or cared about. I know where I would be if he hadn't stepped in when he had. It would look a lot like the ruin you've been wallowing in."

"Nice."

"True," he asserted. "And your situation is my fault. I don't claim to be anything but self-interested, but even I have my limits. Your mother called me family." His profile flexed with his effort to resist some intense emotion. "You're supposed to be able to trust your family to support you, not leave you in harm's way, which is what I did."

"She didn't say that to obligate you!"

"Because she doesn't realize the harm *she's* in. Instead, she feels—sincerely—that there's something in me worth caring about, the same way your damned brother did. That's why I'm so ashamed of letting her down. And him."

He was radiating the coiled energy of a lion with a thorn in his paw, but she was getting the sense this was about more than a twinge of disloyalty to his friend. How could he not think he was worth caring about? She cared about him. She always had.

How to make him see that, though? Without getting rejected again?

There was a knock at the outer door, startling her.

"The jeweler. At least look at what he's brought."

CHAPTER TEN

ELOISE WAS STILL distracted by that glimpse into Konstantin's psyche as she followed him out to the sitting room.

He let in the jeweler who introduced himself as Girard Pascal. He was somewhere in his thirties and very handsome in a tailored blue suit that set off the dark brown of his complexion. One of his bodyguards stayed outside the door while the other entered and swiftly checked each room before stationing himself against a wall near the door.

The reason for the precaution was obvious once Girard unlocked his case and set out his trays containing millions of euros' worth of diamond jewelry.

"Oh, my." Eloise couldn't help sinking onto the settee, dazzled by the array.

"I can make a custom piece if you don't see anything that suits," Girard offered.

"By tomorrow night?" Konstantin asked as he lowered beside her.

"That would be difficult." Girard closed one eye. "I can definitely resize any of these by tomorrow, though."

"We'll need that. Look at these piano fingers." Konstantin picked up her hand to caress her fingers, then perused the selection. He chose one and slid it onto her finger.

"What do you think?"

Her heart started to thud even before she got a proper look at it. So many long-suppressed notions were raging back to life, all as vivid and insubstantial as the flash of rainbows from the marquis-shaped stone. It had to be five carats and was surrounded by a halo of smaller diamonds. More were set down the sides of the platinum band.

Konstantin left her hand draped over his, lightly grasping her curled fingertips as he tilted their grip, allowing the ring to shoot out its sparks from all angles. It was unique and extravagant and yes, a little loose, but so beautiful, Eloise could hardly speak.

"No? Something else?" Konstantin started to release her.

Her fingers instinctually tightened to keep hold of his hand.

His dark gaze lifted to crash into hers, reaching deep into her soul and wrapping around all those deeply embedded dreams of hers.

If she went through with marrying him, she would give up every vestige of herself to him. She knew she would. She would offer her heart and he would take it and could very easily break it. So very easily.

But there was another hidden, hopeful part of her that wanted to think maybe, just maybe, this was the chance she'd always yearned for. That this could be a real marriage to the only man she'd ever wanted.

"You'll wear this one?" Konstantin prodded gently.

She knew what he was really asking. *Will you marry me?*

She nodded before she realized she was doing it, then her husky voice caught up. "I will."

Her fingers trembled as he lifted her hand to his lips and kissed her knuckles.

As he sent Girard away to size the ring, Konstantin experienced a conflicting tide of reactions. Intense satisfaction was the primary one. He had always seen marriage as an encumbrance, but the rationale for this one kept growing. Along with balancing the karmic scales, he would gain a partner who would suit him in many ways—including sexually.

Contrary to what Eloise seemed to think, he did want her. Very badly, in fact. His desire was like a panting beast inside him, ready to run her to ground if necessary.

Which gave him pause. These overly strong responses she provoked were the reason he'd avoided her. He had known since that long ago Christmas that she was far too capable of disarming him when he least expected it.

He would have to be careful, he cautioned himself, and keep a cool head. But even as he turned back to an empty sitting room, and heard a rustle from her bedroom, his libido leaped with intrigue, frying his brain cells.

No. When he arrived in the open door, he found her rifling through the bags that surrounded the bed.

"Call the maid to unpack everything," he told her.

"I'm looking for the jeans I was wearing this morning. Ghaliya said they would be returned. Good grief, Konstantin." She abandoned one bag and picked up another. "This is more damage than I ever did on a back-to-school shopping spree in Paris."

"What of this soiree of your mother's tomorrow? She said it wasn't fancy. I'll wear a suit?"

"She meant it's not white tie. You'll need a tuxedo. I'll call Ghaliya and tell her I need a gown. Are we really doing this?" she asked with distress, looking up from the bag she was searching.

"The party?"

"Marriage." She rubbed her eyebrow. "I mean, I guess

the engagement will give us time to see if we actually work, but that comes with certain risks."

"Such as?"

"The ones my mother warned me about. If we…" She waved at the bed. "I don't want to be in my father's situation, where I have a baby with someone who has all the money so I get cut out."

"That will never happen." What kind of man did she think he was?

"You don't want children?" She dropped her hand to her side, seeming shocked. Disappointed?

"I meant that I can't see us being in such a bad place that I would refuse to let you see our child. I've never given much thought to having any, to be honest. Not beyond the fact I've been told that I should, as part of my succession plan."

"Who stands to inherit now?" She picked up a different bag and set it on the bed.

"I have a foundation that administers to a number of charities."

"You don't have any other relatives?" She paused. "Who's your emergency contact?"

"My assistant." It had seemed perfectly reasonable until he saw her appalled expression. "Now I'll have you." It was another point in the pro column for marriage. "Why? Where do you stand on children?"

"I've always wanted at least two." She hitched her shoulder self-consciously. "So they would be friends the way Ilias and I were."

A pang struck inside him, similar to nostalgia, but different. It was a glimpse of a future that he suddenly wanted. Which wasn't like him. He didn't *yearn*. Especially for something so nascent and fanciful. He brushed the vision aside.

"We can start on that whenever it suits you."

She had found the jeans and paused in shaking them out. She looked to the bed with consternation. The tension around her eyes denoted genuine apprehension.

His mind flooded with those things she'd said about overbearing men and spiked drinks. His gut knotted up.

"If you have concerns about having sex with me, tell me so we can address it," he said quietly.

"Oh, why do you need to know everything about me?" she asked plaintively, shaking the jeans again.

He ran his tongue over his teeth, aware he needed to proceed delicately, but that wasn't his strong suit.

"The irony isn't lost on me that I've told you flat out I don't like to talk about myself so I can't expect you to be an open book." He did, though. He had a ravenous need to know everything about her, which was strange. "For what it's worth, I've shared more with you in the last few days than I've told anyone in years."

A little choking snort noise came out of her.

He lifted a self-deprecating shoulder. "I don't like the memories that are in my head. Why would I put them in yours?"

Her brow crinkled with concern, which made the inside of his chest itch. He looked to the window so she wouldn't see more than he could stand to reveal.

"If we're going to be married, we'll have to share more with each other than we would with anyone else." That combination of intimacy and intensity already wasn't comfortable. It made his nostrils sting with a sense of threat, which was ridiculous. What was she going to do? Waterboard him into revealing his favorite color? He knew how to set boundaries and would. "But I won't force you to tell me anything you don't want to."

"You'll find out eventually, anyway," she mumbled toward the floor. "So I'll just say it." She was blushing bright red. "I'm a virgin. Okay?"

He had one of those discordant moments where his grasp of English seemed to fail him. Was there a different meaning to that word? Because it didn't compute with his assumptions about her.

"*How* old are you?"

"It's your fault," she threw at him before turning her back on him to sit on the bed and work off her boots.

That took him aback. "How?"

"By being all mysterious and good-looking! You know I had the worst case of puppy love." She kept her back to him as she stood and skimmed her legwear down from beneath her skirt. "You think boys my age held any interest for me when I had *you* on the brain?"

"I wasn't trying to encourage that."

"Yes, I know that," she said in a supremely maddened voice. She stepped into the jeans and gave a little hop. "You rejected me enough times—"

"Because—"

"I *know*." The bunched skirt was whisked away and she finished closing her fly. "It doesn't mean I didn't keep thinking about you. It's not like I wanted to have sex with anyone after Ilias, anyway," she allowed sullenly, turning to face him. "But even when I was at university…" She pinched the bridge of her nose. "When I was just this awful mess and couldn't seem to function, I thought, Konstantin would never want someone like this, and it got me out of bed."

Her words were a punch in the chest. He winced, breathing her name, but maybe it was a plea for her to stop because this hurt. It hurt to think of her struggling and thinking of him and *he hadn't been there*.

"I know that sounds stupid, but I needed something to shoot for. I needed to believe that if I got myself together, then I would see you one day and we'd be on equal footing. You'd finally see me and want a relationship with me. Something real. I wanted you to fall in love with me. Instead, it's *this*." Her hand waved aimlessly, voice cracking. "A convenient marriage for sex because I *don't* have my act together. And that sucks."

Oh, hell. Those weren't tears in her eyes. His stomach dropped.

She moved to the night table and blew her nose, taking a shaken breath.

"I'm realizing that I've been nursing a crush on a man I invented. It wasn't *you*. I don't even know you. Not really. But I do want to have sex with you. Obviously." Her expression flexed with deep vulnerability. "And I've never wanted to have sex with anyone else so…"

So she would accept his terms.

She was right. There was something very flat and disappointing in this bloodless arrangement.

"But it's happening really fast." She had her arms wrapped around her torso, supremely defensive.

"We can wait." They were the hardest words he'd ever spoken. Literally hard. He swallowed.

"Are you mad?"

"No." He could use a beat to assimilate all of this, though. He didn't have a fetish around being anyone's first. A lack of experience with sex was no different than never having jumped out of a plane before. Or eating ice cream. It was something that hadn't been tried before. That's all.

But *he* would be the one to jump out of that plane with

her. To show her how it was done. And he wanted her to love it.

"No, I appreciate your honesty." He did. Even though it was making his head swim. "I need to make some calls."

We can wait.

For how long? Eloise wanted to call the question to his back. How much long*er*?

She didn't have the nerve to ask, unwilling to face yet another rejection.

She barely saw Konstantin until they were ready for her mother's party the next evening. She went back to see Ghaliya about her gown, then they dined at the restaurant where they were interrupted by someone he was loosely acquainted with. Afterward, he went to the gym to workout. She had fallen asleep before he got back.

The next morning, she had a fitting, then spent an hour on video chat with her New York roommate who was using the windfall from Konstantin to move to California. Under Eloise's direction, her roommate whittled Eloise's few possessions down to a small box that their neighbor agreed to post when Eloise had a permanent address.

Then she'd been tied up with Ghaliya again, having her hair and makeup done while Konstantin disappeared to pick up her ring.

When she met him in the sitting room, she was nervously petting the rich velvet of her dark mulberry gown.

"Wow." The flicker of his gaze from her eyebrows to the hem of her gown made her prickle all over.

"It's too much, isn't it? Between my size and the late notice, I didn't have much to choose from." She never would have picked something so sexy. The soft fabric hugged her arms and waist and hips before spilling wide around her legs. The low neckline cut over the top of one shoulder and fell off the other. It was outlined in delicate silver lace that added wintery sparkle.

"I think you look incredible. Will you come here, please?" He picked up the ring box from the table beside the sofa and opened it.

She didn't know why his grave tone made her ankles wobble on the six-inch heels as she moved toward him.

He looked incredible, too. His tuxedo jacket was ivory with a black shawl collar and accentuated his wide shoulders and the taper to his waist and long legs.

When she was eye level with his bowtie, she realized, "It matches my dress."

"I told Ghaliya to find me one that would."

Eloise was absorbing what a cute gesture that was when Konstantin stole a cushion off the sofa and dropped it to the floor. He lowered to one knee upon it.

"What—?" Her voice failed her and she clutched at her closing throat. He couldn't be doing what she thought he was doing.

He held out his hand in a request for hers. "I disappointed you yesterday. I want you to have a better story to tell, when people ask you how I proposed."

She bit her lips together, so touched she couldn't speak, only blink to keep the welling tears in her eyes.

"I've never wanted to marry anyone, Eloise. But I want to marry you. That is the truth. Will you marry me?"

He sounded so sincere, her vision blurred. "You're going to make me ruin my makeup," she said on a sniff.

"No," he chided and stood to pluck a tissue from the box he must have placed on the end table for exactly this reason. "I really can't bear tears, *glikia mou*. That is something you need to know about me." He touched her chin to tilt her face up and dabbed the tissue into the corners of her eyes, his expression very somber. "I will try not to make you cry. I promise you that. It hurts too much."

"Oh, you're making it impossible to *not*." She stole the tissue and pressed it under her nose, then fanned her eyes, blinking and fighting the press of emotion. "This was really thoughtful." She had to clear the thickness from her throat. "Thank you." In so many ways, this was her dream come true. Could she really complain if it wasn't *exactly* perfect? "I would be honored to marry you, Konstantin."

"Good." He slid the cool ring onto her finger.

It felt heavier this time. Firmer. More real. It made her heart still, but in a good way. As though it came to rest after a long, long journey.

He looped his arms behind her.

Her hands went to his lapels, still nervous, but quivering with delight at having the right to touch him.

She looked up at him, expecting him to kiss her, but he only caressed the edge of her jaw with his bent finger.

"I've just been cautioned not to ruin your makeup." He dipped his head into her throat and nuzzled his lips against her skin.

She gasped and shivered. Her nipples stung and her knees grew weak.

"I like this height." His breath pooled near her ear, fanning the arousal taking hold in her. "But I don't like these earrings."

"No? Why not?" They were oversized gold hoops that she'd chosen so they wouldn't detract from her gown or engagement ring.

"I didn't buy them for you."

"You did actually—oh."

He had another box in his hand. This one held pear-shaped yellow sapphires dangling from round diamond studs.

"Now I just feel spoiled," she admonished.

"Good. That's what I'm aiming for."

She didn't know what to make of that. Her hand shook as she changed out the earrings.

"Thank you," she murmured as she moved to the mirror and touched the weight of each one, ensuring they were secure. "They're beautiful."

"So are you."

This was surreal. Too perfect. Like a Christmas miracle.

Not that she believed in such things, but maybe, just for tonight, she could.

A hush fell over the crowd as they entered the party. The wall between the front parlor and the great room had been opened and the furniture moved to the sides, creating a ballroom. While her mother and Antoine greeted them at the entrance, everyone paused to smiled and offer a polite round of applause.

"I've shared your exciting news with our guests," her mother said cheerily. "Oh, you look beautifully festive, darling." She stepped back from pressing their cheeks to admire her gown. "And, Konstantin. You've made me the happiest woman in the world."

"I could have sworn I did that, *ma chère*," Antoine said smoothly, but Eloise heard the edge in his tone. He caught Eloise's hand, bringing it up so he could inspect the ring with a cynical curl to his lip. His gaze touched her earlobe before drilling into hers. "Buttering all sides of your bread, I see."

"I thought you'd be pleased to see me make such an advantageous match. For the family," she added with a saccharine smile and subtly tried to extricate her hand from his grip.

His hold tightened, not painful, but to show her that he would decide when to let her go, not her. After a charged second of warning, he released her and shook Konstantin's hand before turning his attention to whoever was coming in behind them.

Fresh nerves attacked when they moved into the heart of the party.

As the daughter of Lilja Drakos and the sister of Ilias Drakos, Eloise had always been accepted—maybe *tolerated* was a better word—by her mother's peers. She was illegitimate and only a half sister to the heir of the Drakos fortune, not in line for any money of her own, so she'd never deserved much attention, good or bad. Which suited her. She wasn't built for notoriety.

Konstantin was very well-known, of course. He hadn't been kidding when he had claimed she would have influence as his wife, either. Even as his just-announced intended, she had more cache than she'd ever imagined. People who would, in the past, expect her to come to them, were suddenly coming forward to congratulate them, vying for her attention and an introduction to her powerful husband.

They circulated for well over an hour, making small talk and deflecting prying questions. It was a relief when her mother and Antoine finally started the dancing, taking the attention off them.

Then Konstantin took her in his arms and Eloise was aware of only him and the music, nothing else. His hands were sure on her, his steps smooth and perfectly on tempo. The solidness of his shoulder and the brush of his thighs and the fading spice of his aftershave all put her into a spell where she let herself believe, just for a moment, that her life was turning out exactly as she had always wanted it to.

"Are you going to play?" Konstantin asked.

"Hmm?" She lifted her gaze to see he was looking toward the piano where a serious young man in wire-rimmed glasses and a suit vest over striped trousers was mastering the instrument. "No." The ensemble of five was expertly moving from background classical to waltzes and contemporary instrumentals, interspersing them with a few Christmas carols. "Having an audience was always my stumbling block. I had ten years of classical lessons so I can get through a performance if I have to, but I don't enjoy playing for crowds. I do it for me. If someone wants to sit down and listen, that's their business."

"Is that why therapy appeals? Because it's about the individual?"

"Yes, exactly!" She looked up at him, pleased to be understood. "Oh."

"What's wrong?" He pivoted her out of her small misstep.

"Nothing. Only that we were under the mistletoe—"

"Were we?" He twirled her back, forcing another couple to make a quick turn to avoid them. When they were directly below the dangling ornament of berries in the middle of the floor, he said, "What do we do now?"

"I think you know," she said with amusement twitching her lips.

"I do," he agreed and cupped the side of her face as he dropped his head to press his mouth over hers.

From the outside, it probably looked chaste, but it was a lingering, sensual kiss that subtly claimed her, curling her toes and making her pulse trip. She let her eyelids flutter closed and melted against him.

When a ripple of amused *aahs* rose around them, he drew back, obsidian eyes filled with banked heat.

"Shall we switch?" Antoine appeared beside them with her mother. A new song started.

Konstantin's expression cooled, but he found a warmer look for Lilja.

"I would be honored." And it would be expected that her fiancé dance with his future mother-in-law while Antoine took Eloise for a spin.

The tempo was a foxtrot and Antoine was a good dancer, leading her expertly through the steps while saying with quiet malice, "You don't really expect me to believe this charade?"

She didn't bother playing dumb. "Edoardo wanted to marry me. Why wouldn't Konstantin?"

"Because I sweetened the pot for Edoardo. What could you possibly offer a man like Konstantin? That you're not already giving up," Antoine added scathingly. "Or is that how you got the ring? By holding out on him? That will only work so long, girlie. He won't go through with marrying you. What could he possibly gain?"

She didn't want be so withered by his words, but he was giving voice to the insecurity she already felt. Maybe Konstantin was only intrigued by the sex they weren't yet having. She might not be any good at it, for all she knew. And beyond that, all she offered him was a chance for him to feel he was squaring things with her dead brother. He had already mentioned divorce and turned away from her more times than she cared to count.

Not that she revealed any of that to Antoine. She kept it to a stiff, "I'm not here to prove anything to you. I just wanted to see my mother."

"You want her ring. And for her to pay for a wedding

and all the parties and frills that go with it. I won't let that happen. Get what you can out of Galanis. That's no skin off my nose, but don't come crawling back here when he throws you out."

Whether it was a newfound boldness that came from knowing Konstantin was in her corner or an old spark of her former self, before life had delivered so many blows, Eloise threw back her head and said, "I haven't wanted to make my mother choose between her husband and her child, but do you honestly believe she would pick you if I did?"

"She already did," he said with a cruel tilt to his mouth.

The music stopped and Eloise was close enough to the edge of the dance floor that she melted into the crowd, but her pulse was pounding in her ears and her hair felt as though it would catch fire any second.

"What did he say to you?" Konstantin asked grimly, coming up behind her where she was accepting a glass of wine from a bartender.

"Nothing," she lied.

"You might hide how you feel about him from your mother, but not from me. What did he say?" he repeated through clenched teeth.

She glanced up and felt incredibly defenseless, not just because he read her so easily, but because of the things Antoine had said.

"He thinks I'm using our engagement to get Mom to go back to paying for my lavish lifestyle. He said she's already chosen him over me."

"I've had it with him." Konstantin turned his head to search over the heads of the crowd. "Are you ready to leave?"

"Yes, but—" She set aside her glass and touched his

arm to keep him from walking away. "You're not going to make a scene, are you?"

"No. I'm going to make a point." He took her hand and wound her through the crowd to where her mother and Antoine were speaking to another couple. "Lilja. Thank you for inviting us, but we have an early departure for Greece tomorrow. We're calling it a night. Are you sure we can't persuade you to spend Christmas with us?"

"I'm tempted. I miss Athens."

"We're going to Como for the holiday," Antoine said firmly. "Lilja has been looking forward to it."

"And we're going to Crete," Konstantin said, still speaking to her mother. "But we'll have the wedding in Athens if that's easier for you. I'll fly to Como and kidnap you myself if I have to."

"That won't be necessary. We're only staying until the second. Eloise." Lilja touched the large emerald pendant dangling from the thick gold chain around her throat. "You're *not* marrying on Christmas Day."

"No." She sent an alarmed look to Konstantin. *Were they?*

"Much to my dismay, there's a seven-day waiting period in Greece," Konstantin said. "So it will be the twenty-eighth or ninth. I'll let you know once we've finalized everything. You and I have a lot to cover before then." Konstantin finally swung his attention to Antoine who was looking like he'd been kicked in the peanuts. "Expect paperwork first thing in the morning."

"You're marrying in a *week*?"

"Konstantin. We need a year," her mother protested before she sent a startled look to Eloise. "Are you pregnant?"

"*No.*"

"Oh." Her mother pouted. "That's too bad. A grandchild would have been icing on the wedding cake, but, Konstantin—" she touched his sleeve "—I only have one daughter. I want her to have the perfect wedding."

"So do I. You and Eloise may spend as much of my money as you want, on a ceremony as extravagant as you want, on whichever day you want to have it, but I am making Eloise my wife before the year ends." He wove their fingers together. "That is nonnegotiable."

"He reminds me more and more of Petros by the minute," Lilja confided with amusement to Eloise. "I wouldn't dream of missing your big wedding day, darlings. Melissa will understand our leaving Como early. I can't wait to tell her. How exciting!" Lilja hugged them both again. "Have a lovely Christmas. We'll see you both in a few days."

CHAPTER ELEVEN

"A WEEK?" ELOISE BUSTLED ahead of him into their hotel sitting room, sounding agitated. "When did you decide that?"

"When I found out the waiting period was a week," he drawled. "It's a month here in France. Would you rather marry tomorrow? We could fly to Gibraltar." *Say yes*, he willed.

"But why are you in such a hurry?" Her skirt billowed as she whirled and face him. "To put pressure on Antoine?" She was fiddling with her ring, looking anxious, so he took a moment to consider how his words might land.

"I thought my motive was obvious." He shrugged out of his tuxedo jacket and loosened his bowtie. "When you said you're a virgin, I presumed we'd wait until our wedding night. I don't want to wait a year to make love to you. It's all I can do to wait a week."

She started to say something, hesitated, then blurted, "Do *I* have any say in that?"

"You have all the say in that. Why? Is that too fast?"

Her gaze skittered away from his, chin setting belligerently, and he was overcome by the most tender delight.

"Or is it too slow?" he asked knowingly.

"Don't make me feel embarrassed for it!" she said crossly.

"How exactly do you feel?" He padded toward her, trying not to be smug, but damn this reaction of hers was satisfying. "Are you impatient? You seemed nervous when we talked about it yesterday."

"I'm terrified," she admitted, letting her hand alight on the pleats of his shirtfront before she jerked it back as though scorched. "What if it's awful? And then we're stuck with each other? Do you really want that? To go into marriage blind?"

"Now your inexperience really is showing." He took her hand and lightly tugged an invitation to move closer. "There's no chance of it being awful. We have incredible chemistry, Eloise. That's why you melt every time I touch you."

She was doing it now, leaning into him, but fighting it. He tried to rub the tension from her shoulder blades.

"It's not the same for you, though," she mumbled into his shirt. "You don't feel this helpless. Do you?" Her brows came together crossly.

"No, I feel powerful. Like I'm holding the sun." He brought her hand to the back of his neck and trailed his touch down the velvet that covered her arm. She shivered and caught her breath. He smiled. "It's intoxicating. Exciting."

"That doesn't sound equal. It sounds like you're in control and I'm not."

"But how does it *feel*?" he chided as he shifted the velvet of her gown against her, rubbing the slippery silk lining against her skin.

He definitely liked her in high heels. When she let her head fall back, her mouth was right there for the slant of his.

The taste of her sent a sweep of heat through him, like a sip of fine scotch. He wanted to get drunk on her. To gulp her down, but therein lay the danger. He had to keep some control in this.

Still, as he made himself lift his head and say, "I'm going to shower," he couldn't resist adding, "I won't lock the door. Join me if you want to."

He left her with heat searing from her lips to the pit of her belly. With a sense of being abandoned, but of wanting to abandon herself.

Take me, she thought.

But he wanted something that was infinitely more difficult. He wanted her to give herself to him. That took bravery and trust. It might even cost her soul.

But he was already in possession of it.

Was she being a complete fool? How well did she really know him? Barely at all! Her brother had trusted him and Konstantin felt a compelling debt toward Ilias, but what did he feel for *her*? Nothing so deep as what she felt toward him.

It made the act of going to him more than just a conscious decision. It was a huge risk, but she wanted to believe that if she had the courage to take this step, she might find the deeper regard and loving relationship she was looking for.

She kicked off her shoes and walked on unsteady legs into his room, dropping her gown to the floor along the way. She came up against the cracked door where she could hear the quiet rustle of clothing. She slowly pushed it open.

He turned from hanging his trousers on a hook, naked but for the snug black underwear that outlined his erection straining the front. His gaze ate up her powder-pink strapless bra and matching lace cheekies while she admired the bronzed cast that was his chest and muscled shoulders and tense abdomen.

His attention came back to her face and he said, "I should have got the pink ones."

She touched her ear. "I should, um…" She removed her jewelry, leaving it in the empty soap dish with her hairpins. Then she used a couple of the complementary makeup removal wipes, aware of him standing so close she could feel the heat off his body, but he didn't touch her.

"You're not going to start the shower?" she asked as she dropped the little pads into the bin.

"I'm enjoying watching you. And don't be mad when I say this, but I'm surprised how short you are."

She dipped her chin in warning.

"It's because you have a very sunny personality. I saw it tonight. You make people smile and when you tell a story, people want to hear it. It makes you seem bigger than you are. I think that's why I didn't recognize you right away in New York. I genuinely remembered you taller than you really are."

"Thank you, I guess?" she said wryly.

"I mean it as a compliment. I hate parties and you made tonight bearable."

"That's another compliment? Maybe if we workshop them before delivery."

His mouth twitched. "See, like that. You're funny and engaging."

He leaned into the shower and wrenched the taps on. As the hiss of the water filled the room and the air grew so thick it was hard to breath, he very casually skimmed down his underwear and stepped out of them, then straightened to his full intimidating height. His erection jutted out, unabashed.

"Let's not waste water," he chided, and nodded at her to finish stripping.

Her stomach pitched with nerves as she reached behind herself to release her bra, letting it fall to the floor before she rolled her cheekies down her legs, too shy to look at him as she stepped out of them.

He held the door for her like a gentleman, then followed her into the cubicle.

It wasn't the spacious shower of his New York penthouse and she didn't have it all to herself. This one was big enough for two, but just barely. His body brushed hers beneath the spray and his arm grazed her breast when he reached for the soap. He rolled the bar between his hands, then he slid his soapy hands over her skin, dragging her close and planting a wet hungry kiss across her mouth.

A glorious rush pulsed through her. She gave in to her wicked, greedy urge to slick her hands over his sides and back and up to his shoulders, then rubbed her breasts against the lather in the fine hairs on his chest and welcomed his tongue with the brush of her own.

He groaned and pressed her into the cool tiles. There was a dull thud of the soap falling. His hands covered her breasts, massaging and flicking her nipples in a way that sent wires of electric heat deep between her thighs, making her writhe.

His erection was a thick insistent shape against her abdomen and she started to touch him, then hesitated.

"Go ahead," he rasped, easing back enough that she could stroke the steely shape of him.

"Show me?" she asked shyly.

He wrapped his hand over hers and crushed her fist around his girth, moving in her hand as she began to stroke

him. She was fascinated and smugly pleased when he closed
his eyes and bit out a ragged curse.

He leaned down to kiss her, saying against her mouth, "I
can feel you smiling. Do you think I'll let you take me over
the edge without you?" His hand slid down her abdomen
and between her thighs, capturing her mound in a possessive cup that pooled water against her flesh, rinsing away
the soap before his touch delved into her folds.

Despite the lack of lather, his fingertips slid easily
against her aroused flesh. She gasped at the stark intimacy
of it, the sensitivity and sparking points of pleasure.

"What if we're not good together?" he mocked and
probed lightly against her entrance. "Do you want this?"

"Yes," she whispered, not even sure what to expect, only
knowing that she wanted *more*. More pleasure. More intimacy. More of him.

His long finger penetrated her. It wasn't painful, but it
was strangely intense. Deeply personal, then…

"Oh…" she groaned as he played his thumb across the
bundle of nerves that sent pleasure thrumming through
her whole being.

"Squeeze me tight," he urged against the corner of her
mouth.

She didn't know if he meant with her hand or her body,
but she was nothing but tension from head to toe, making noises that echoed off the walls of the shower while
he danced his touch into her body and against her clit. She
gave him her tongue and moved with him, wallowing in
how sexy and smutty and *good* it felt.

Then she was teetering at the pinnacle. He held her bottom lip in a gentle scrape of his teeth while his dark eyes
turned midnight black.

The tension inside her released in a sudden rush of contractions. She might have been embarrassed by how quickly she'd fallen apart, but he was tilting back his head, groaning at the ceiling while the water rained down and he pulsed in her hand.

After they dried off, he left her in his bed with a lingering kiss, saying, "I need to make some calls."

"It's midnight." She felt like butter and wanted to melt herself all over his toasty form.

"Not in Australia. That's where your mother's trustee retired to." He pulled on the trousers he'd been wearing earlier in the day. "I want to speak to some of my Sydney people about locating him. I don't know if he has ties to Antoine so they need to be delicate."

"Oh." She had thought they might continue making love. Was he being chivalrous or had she done something wrong?

"Sleep. I'll join you soon." He rose and walked out.

She tried to stay awake, but all the travel and stress must have caught up to her. She was deeply asleep when she realized Konstantin was rolling away from spooning behind her, leaving the bed.

"What's wrong?" she asked drowsily, completely disoriented by the sound of him zipping into his trousers. Hadn't he done that already?

"Some genius ordered the maid to come early so she could pack up all your new clothes." His voice was graveled with sleep. "Our flight plan is filed for nine."

"Oh." She couldn't help grimacing. "Are you the genius?"

"I am the genius."

She desperately wanted to duck under the blanket and sleep longer, but as he closed the door she heard him let the maid into the sitting room. She threw off the covers and hurried into the bathroom so she could steal the robe off the back of the door.

The rest of the morning was taken up by travel. They flew straight to Crete, landing in Heraklion before they transferred into a helicopter that hopped them to Konstantin's mountaintop villa.

It was a spectacular estate, especially when viewed from above. The house sprawled in decadent white wings with pretty balconies and windows that reflected sky and sea. There was a courtyard with a pergola of vines over it and a broad terrace with a pool set into it like a jewel. The roof was covered in solar panels and the surrounding hillsides were skirted with vineyards and olive groves amid the broken walls of ancient ruins.

The path from the helicopter pad toward the house was flanked in bougainvillea and potted citrus trees struggling to bloom in the cool temperatures of December.

A stocky young man hurried out to greet them, black curly hair cut very short, glasses slightly askew.

"*Kýrie… Kyría*," he greeted, adding in heavily accented English, "Once again, I must apologize for the confusion with the rooms in Nice."

"It's done," Konstantin dismissed. "Eloise, this is Nemo, assistant to my EA. I was expected to be on vacation, so I've been leaning heavily on him this week."

"I'm honored to meet you, *kyría*. Welcome to Greece. My number is in your phone. Please call or text me with anything I can do to make you more comfortable here."

"I was born in Athens," she said in Greek. "I'm already very comfortable here."

"You speak Greek?" Konstantin snapped his attention to her. "Why have we been speaking English?"

"I'm rusty," she excused with a shrug. "I didn't want to embarrass myself. I'll brush up now that I'm here, though."

"You certainly will," Konstantin muttered. In Greek.

Nemo looked between them, not sure if he was supposed to be amused.

"Please come meet Filomena," he decided to say. "She's the niece of the regular housekeeper who is on vacation. She has a young family so she can only come in for a few hours each morning. I've contacted an agency if you'd like someone here full-time?"

"Mornings are fine," Konstantin said to the young woman when they found her putting away groceries in the kitchen. "Thank you for coming on short notice."

"Of course." She smiled shyly at both of them.

"Oh, this is beautiful," Eloise said as they moved from the expansive kitchen out to the living area.

The decor was soothing grays and muted earth tones, picking up the colors of the marble floor and contrasting against the white walls. Beyond the abundant windows, the terrace and pool sat against a screen of endless blue sea and scudding clouds. Eloise was drawn outside to the covered dining area where she was protected from the bite of the damp wind.

Inside, she heard Konstantin say, "When can we expect the—wait. Let it be a surprise for Eloise, since it's for her. When will it arrive?"

"This afternoon," Nemo assured him. "And where… um…?" He smiled uncertainly as Eloise came back inside, drawn by curiosity. "Where would you like me to put it?"

"Here." Konstantin waved at a cozy seating area next to the fireplace, where she could imagine herself curling up to read a book and sip a glass of wine.

"Are you getting a tree?" Eloise guessed, warmed that

he would indulge her like that. "You don't have to do that for me if it's not something you usually have."

"The tree will be here tonight," Nemo said, faltering in a brief way that suggested to Eloise that he was expecting more than a tree. "Filomena's husband will bring it. She looked for decorations in the storage room, but couldn't find any."

"I don't have any," Konstantin said.

"I'll pick some up later and hang them tonight. Do you have a color preference?" Nemo asked Eloise.

"You probably don't know, but I happen to be one of Santa's helpers." Eloise splayed her hand on her chest. "As such, I would love to buy decorations and hang them. It sounds like you have enough to do."

"It's no trouble for me." Nemo looked to Konstantin for guidance, seeming anxious not to step on her toes, but nor was he about to shirk his duties.

"We'll go into the village and see what we can find," Konstantin said, adding ironically, "So Santa can get his sled in here without being seen."

"Konstantin, I haven't even got you *one* gift," Eloise protested, growing anxious as she suspected something else was planned. Her finances did not run to plane fare and sapphire earrings and whatever else he was planning, either. Buying a few baubles for the tree would be a strain.

"I don't need anything," Konstantin said dismissively. "Except thirty minutes to finish speaking with Nemo. Please tell Filomena we'll find dinner while we're out. She doesn't need to prepare anything." He turned back to Nemo. "Come into my office and tell me where we are with the lawyers."

Eloise delivered her message, but Filomena wouldn't let

her help in the kitchen or let her carry up the luggage that the pilot had left on a cart in the breezeway.

"Nemo and I will unpack it while you're out," she promised.

She told Eloise where to shop for decorations, but didn't have any suggestions for a gift for Konstantin. "My husband enjoys assembling model planes and fishing so I always have options in that vein."

Did Konstantin have hobbies? Eloise didn't know, which was an uncomfortable reminder that she was marrying a man who was still a mystery to her. One who had made her feel divine, then left her in the bed and walked away, not seeming nearly as affected by their interlude in the shower as she had been.

He had also delivered her back to her mother and put her stepfather on notice. She wanted to show her gratitude for that. She had to give him something and it had to be meaningful.

She picked up her phone to search *inexpensive gifts for men*, but was struck by the perfect idea before she'd unlocked her screen.

She hurried back to the kitchen to ask Filomena where she could find what she needed.

Konstantin parked the Jeep in one of the spots facing the beach, then walked around to wrap his arm around Eloise, trying to protect her from the gust of salt-scented wind.

"Do you want to get a coffee?" Eloise asked as they reached the stoop of a *kafeneio*.

"Sure." He used his free hand to reach for the door, but her words halted him.

"Good. Stay here while I nip out for something."

"What is it?" He flexed his arm, keeping her beside him. "I can go."

"Filomena told me where I could get your gift."

"No, thank you." He held onto her as she tried to slip away from him and leave the stoop.

"What do you mean *no thank you*?" She scraped at a tendril of hair that the breeze whipped across her face. "It's for Christmas."

"I told you I don't need anything. But let's get coffee. We can drink it while we shop. It won't feel so cold once we're in the alleys." He started to open the door again.

She dug in her heels. "Konstantin. You didn't ask me if I wanted three thousand gifts in four days. You just gave them to me."

"Because they're things I want you to have."

She said nothing, only stared pointedly at him.

"I don't like receiving gifts," he admitted, shifting so he was at least forming a buffer against the wind, protecting her from it.

"Why not?"

In his mind's eye, he saw a toy sailboat hit the stones of the chimney, smashing into pieces. "I just don't like it."

"So the gift you refuse to give me is the gift of giving you a gift?" she challenged.

"Yes."

The amusement in her gaze turned searching. Troubled.

"It's a lot of secrets and subterfuge. For what?" He tried to downplay it.

"It's fun. Otherwise, you would tell me what's being delivered while we're out."

He didn't want to tell her. He wanted to see her reaction when they got home and found it there.

"I'm not getting you dance lessons or an ugly tie, I

swear," she cajoled. "It's just something small that I want you to have because I don't think you do. I think you'll like it."

That was the issue. If he did like it, and revealed that, it could be used against him.

She wasn't like that. He knew she wasn't. But there was still a hard wall inside him that wanted to stay firm and strong against even the possibility of cruelty.

She looked so earnest, though.

He sighed shortly. "It's really that important to you?"

"I could have bought it by now if we hadn't been arguing about it all this time."

"Go, then. Be back in ten minutes or I'm coming to look for you."

He went inside to order coffee, then he sat at one of the outdoor tables, watching up the street for her to return, irritated with himself for being so churlish with her.

He'd been feeling off-balance since their shower last night. The sex hadn't been adventurous, but it had been intimate enough and powerful enough that he'd needed some time to put himself back together afterward.

Thankfully, she'd been fast asleep when he came to bed or he would have made love with her. He wanted to. Physically, his body was craving hers the way vampires craved blood, but on a more psychic level she was churning up his equilibrium.

He kept himself closed off for a reason, trying not to ruin lives through deliberate negligence, but otherwise he took little responsibility for how others felt. Eloise was different. Every emotion that emanated from her sifted through him in some way. If she seemed distressed, he wanted to remove the reason for it. If she smiled, he felt it like a thousand rays of sunshine bursting into life within him.

This growing attachment to her grated most of all, warning him that he was developing an Achilles' heel.

If he were honest with himself, he would admit that she'd always been one. It was only widening now that he was spending time with her, encompassing more and more of him as he allowed her to get closer.

Damn it, he'd forgotten to ask if she needed money.

He tapped his pocket to ensure he had his phone and wallet as he rose to stand, but there she was, walking toward him. If she had purchased something, it was in the shoulder bag she had brought with her.

"Cream, one sugar," he said, offering the take-out cup of coffee he'd ordered for her.

"Thank you." She sipped and closed her eyes. "Mmm… Greek coffee. My one true love."

Not me?

The whimsical words hovered on his tongue. He bit them back, but wondered where the urge to say them had come from. He wasn't jealous of coffee. Was he?

"Filomena said there's a shop with a green awning that would have decorations. I think I saw it when I passed that alley back there."

They shopped for the next hour, picking out garlands and ornaments and a centerpiece for the table, then ordered sweet and savory treats from the bakery to be delivered the next day. After leaving their purchases in the Jeep, they went into a nearby taverna where they sat by a window overlooking the wharf.

"We should walk out there after dinner. I always loved seeing the boats decorated with lights." Eloise cupped her hands around the *tsikoudia*-spiked toddy she'd ordered and smiled across the steam that rose from the mug. "Ilias would buy cookies and we'd eat them on the beach while

we watched boats go by. It was one of our Christmas traditions. Thank you for today. This is the first year without
him that I've felt the least bit interested in celebrating."

"You're welcome," he said, mildly amused that she was
expressing more gratitude over glass ornaments and strings
of lights than she had for the designer clothes or sapphire
earrings he'd given her.

It had been a pleasant afternoon, though. More enjoy-
able that he would have expected. He put his mellow mood
down to the warmed shot of raki with honey, cinnamon and
clove he was nursing.

"What sorts of traditions did you have, growing up?"
she asked.

"None," he dismissed and looked to the menu neither of
them had read yet. "Should we have the *stifado*?" It was a
rustic beef stew made with red wine and tomato. "It seems
to be their specialty."

"That sounds good. Thank you." She waited while he
waved over the server and ordered, then said, "I'm sorry,
Konstantin. I didn't realize that you don't celebrate Christmas. I presumed you were culturally Christian if not prac-
ticing. Do you observe something else?"

"No."

"Then why…?" She frowned with puzzlement.

He came up against the contradiction where he preferred
not to discuss his past, but saw that it would be more practical to make his explanation so he would never have to
talk about it again. "It's nothing to do with religion. When
I was very young, there wasn't any money for birthdays or
Christmas. If we had a good meal on any day of the year,
that was celebration enough. After my mother was gone,
neither my grandfather nor I had much interest in any of
the holidays so I've never observed them."

"What about when you were at school? We always had a year-end party and exchanged gifts in our dorms. You didn't do things like that?"

"The other boys did." They would buzz with talk of where their family would travel to ski or see relatives, excited by what they hoped to find under the tree. "Some would pester me to draw a name, but there were a handful of other boys who didn't celebrate for whatever reason. It was easy enough to opt out."

"Ilias never gave you any gifts?" She couldn't believe that.

"Video games," he said drily, under no illusion as to his friend's motive. "So I could be coerced into playing them with him."

"He was always sneaky like that, wasn't he?"

He was. And he would look at Konstantin with an expression like hers, too. Not pitying exactly, but earnest and fretful, wanting to pull him into the group. Wanting him to experience a high that Konstantin knew would only put him in danger of a fall.

"You don't miss what you've never had," he said in a tone of finality.

She flinched, which he regretted, but their stew arrived so it was easy enough to close the subject and move on to other things.

CHAPTER TWELVE

ELOISE WANTED TO respect Konstantin's privacy around his childhood. He had said he didn't talk about how he had come to live with his grandfather and, given the small glimpses he'd offered of his past, she suspected there was a great deal of pain and sadness along with poverty and a certain amount of neglect.

It made her heart hurt to think of it, but it helped her understand why he was so remote and unused to small gestures of kindness. She couldn't stop thinking about that remark he'd made the other day about not thinking he was worth caring about. Did he really feel that way? It made her wonder if he even believed in love or would ever offer her his heart.

What did that mean for their marriage if he was so closed off?

She was lost in introspection when they arrived back at the villa. They paused to hang their coats and put on the slippers Filomena had left for them, then moved into the great room with their purchases. Filomena had gone home and Nemo was staying in the pool house so the villa was empty. Eloise looked for the tree that—

"Oh, my God!" she cried as the Steinway piano hit her eyeballs. A giant red bow sat atop the closed lid. "You didn't? Oh, my God, Konstantin. Oh, my *God*." She wanted to *hug* it.

She spun to hug him instead, but craned her neck to stare at the piano through eyes that blurred with tears.

"You're shaking," he said with amusement as he rubbed her back. "It's okay. It's real."

"I'm just so—" She turned her face into his shirt, trying to dry her face since tears disturbed him, but they were overflowing anyway. She'd missed playing *so much*.

"You're not crying. Eloise, *no*." He sounded agonized as he cupped the side of her face and used his thumb to wipe her cheek. "This was supposed to make you happy."

"I'm ecstatic." She could hardly speak she was so overwhelmed. She ran her trembling fingers under her eyes. "I know I should say it's too much and you shouldn't have. I won't even call it mine. I'm just happy to see it and play it. I'm never going to leave here. I hope you know that. I'm going to sit right there for the rest of my life." She pointed at the bench.

"Then who will play the ones I've ordered for Athens and New York?"

"No!" she squealed, slipping into gales of laughter because there was no other way to let the joy burst out of her. She clutched her fists into his cable-knit pullover and leaned into him, so overcome she couldn't process it.

"You're being silly," he scolded as he kept her from collapsing weakly to the floor.

"*I'm* being silly?" That was even funnier. That grand piano was worth six figures and he was buying them by the dozen, like eggs. Her shoulder's hurt, she was laughing so hard.

"Are you going to play with your new toy, or not?" He

was trying to sound stern, but there was a big smile on his face and *that* nearly broke her.

She'd never seen him smile, not like that. Not with his whole face so he looked carefree and star-power handsome, with a glint in his dark eyes and creases beside his mouth.

She reached up to urge him to dip his head so she could kiss him.

His arms tightened across her back, holding her as he arched over her, making her tingle to her toes as he immediately took over the kiss, consuming her for several wild heartbeats before he straightened and set her on her feet.

"Go," he said huskily. "The tuner was here when they set it up. I want to know if he needs to come back."

She had a feeling he was trying to tamp down on his own emotions, but she was torn between the dual desires to touch the piano and touch him. She was dizzy as she moved toward the instrument, still buzzing with sensuality and now growing anticipation and absolute delight. She flexed her fingers as she sat, then lifted the fallboard. Her hands found her warm-up scales and it sounded perfect.

"Don't judge my mistakes. I'm out of practice." Especially for a masterpiece that she hadn't played since relearning it for her audition to the therapy program earlier this year. It suited this occasion, though.

She began picking out the first notes of Beethoven's "Ode to Joy."

As she did, Konstantin came to stand behind her. He rested his hands on her shoulders, sending a force down her arms that felt electric. She flubbed a couple of notes and kept going, feeling more alive than she ever had in her life.

Konstantin carefully drew her hair tie from her ponytail while she cheated her way through the most complex chords, then sifted his fingers through the length as she poured her elation into the keys.

As the emotion built, then softened, then built again, his light touch caressed her nape and into her throat, making her breasts tighten.

Her shoulder brushed his fly and she realized he was hard, but she continued to race her fingers across the keys, chasing the flights of notes.

It was like they were having sex, folding feeling onto tension, building one on the other in thicker and thicker layers. She wanted that. She wanted sex. She wanted Konstantin. She wanted to feel this wild intensity inside her while *he* was inside her, driving her up and up and up to the heights and then...

The finale. She held that chord soaked with carnal yearning, allowing it to resonate through the room, from her body into his.

His hand slid lower to fondle her braless breast. She arched into his cupping touch, tilting her head back. He swooped to kiss her, drawing her off the bench and kneeing it aside as he pressed her against the piano. Her backside hit the keys in a discordant hum as he kissed the hell out of her.

She had wanted this for years, this hunger that was pouring out of him as though he were starved for her. It was so much more than she had imagined. Wilder. More dominating, more all-encompassing. It probably should have alarmed her, but this craving of his was everything she wanted. The love she'd always had for him was maturing as they spent these days together. It expanded further as he kissed her with unfettered passion. She didn't know how else to express her feelings except to kiss him back with the same ferocious energy.

As she looped her arms around his neck, he scooped

her up and lifted her onto the piano so she was more eye
to eye with him. His gleaming gaze was atavistic, his features tense and flushed with lust.

Had she done this to him? It was thrilling. She cupped
the sides of his head and spoke against his mouth. "I want
to make love."

"Lie back."

"I meant—"

"I know what you meant. We'll get there. But I've been
thinking about this since I saw you play 'I'm Coming for
Christmas.'"

"That's not what it's called."

"I know. Lie back." There was a twitch of amusement
at the corner of his mouth.

"Hilarious." But she actually did think it was funny.
"Careful," she added as he pulled her hips closer to the
edge. "My jeans might scratch the finish."

"Then we should remove them."

A nervous quivering invaded her abdomen as she settled on her back and opened her fly. When he grabbed the
waistband in his fists, she lifted her hips and let him drag
them away, only realizing as the cool air hit her damp folds
that he'd taken her underwear with them.

As her bare backside settled on the cool maple, his hands
ran up her naked legs, claiming her thighs firmly and pushing them open.

"I—" She shyly tried to find leverage to close them,
stepping on a few keys that plinked.

"Let me," he said, hot breath stirring the fine hairs on
her mound, increasing the unsteadiness deep in her belly.

His fingers tickled and trailed around her outer folds,
stimulating her. Teasing until heat gathered there with
dampness and throbs of need. Then his touch grew more

intimate, exploring and exposing her. When anticipation was coiled in her abdomen and she was biting her lip with yearning, the first lick of his tongue landed with such sensitive precision she jerked and tried to sit up.

There was no escaping what he did to her, though. He hugged her thigh and buried his mouth against her tender flesh, swirling and sweeping her into such a state of intense pleasure that she could hardly bear it.

Before she knew it, she was hooking her heel into his back, lifting to increase the pressure, seeking the culmination that was building inexorably inside her. She was filling the room with more song than the piano, moaning with pleasure and tight sobs of need.

When he eased one finger, then two inside her, it was the tipping point. Her moans turned to cries as climax shuddered through her, arching her back and twisting powerful contractions through her that sent flushes of heat chasing through her whole body.

He slowed his clever ministrations, soothing now as the rocketing pulses slowed and faded, leaving her limp and splayed before him.

"That was exquisite," he said in a rasp that abraded all her sensitized nerves in the best possible way.

She was still weak with gratification, all inhibition gone, feeling so dreamy she couldn't move except to roll her head and watch him nuzzle the crease of her thigh.

"This is the happiest day of my life."

"Ha!" He picked up his head and gave her position of abandonment a thorough, possessive study. "Mine, too." He gathered her up and turned to the stairs.

The upper floor was a his-and-hers suite with a shared sitting room and a terrace that could be accessed from all three rooms. Each bedroom had its own walk-in closet and luxurious bathroom.

Eloise had already seen her room with its pastel greens and subtle blue-and-ivory accents. Konstantin's was a stronger palette of navy and forest and silver, all of it muted by the single lamp that was burning against the shadows of night.

The bed met her back before she realized she was tipping. His weight arrived between her thighs in the same motion. He held himself on his elbows and continued to kiss her, hands bracketing her head while his tongue searched out hers, brushing and claiming and wickedly suggesting the lovemaking that was to come.

Her senses were accosted by his weight and heat and the fact her legs were scraping denim as she rubbed her thigh against his. It was erotic to be half clothed this way, making her feel vulnerable against the roughness. She was overwhelmed by his power and size, but when his hand swept under her top and claimed her breast, swooping excitement dove into her belly and heat poured through her loins.

She ran her trembling hands over him, seeking skin beneath his pullover only to come up against his tucked shirt. She bunched the fine fabric in her fist, trying to pull it free of his jeans.

He rose onto his knees and yanked up his pullover, throwing it away before tearing open the buttons of his shirt with impatience.

She sat up to help, crooking her open legs on either side of his as she clumsily slipped the button on his jeans free, then drew his fly down. It took delicate wrangling to wriggle her fingers into denim and briefs, but she managed to reveal the shape pressing so insistently for release.

When she was holding his hot, turgid flesh, she sent one

glance upward and found him watching her intently. Her stomach swooped again.

Nervously, she closed her fist around the root of his shaft and bent forward. It was curiosity and desire and a need to thank him and please him and *love* him.

But she was uncertain. She licked lightly, hearing his breath hiss in, which was encouraging. His fingers combed into her hair and massaged her scalp, encouraging her to continue. She explored his shape more thoroughly, painting him with her tongue until she found the courage to close her lips around his tip to delicately suck.

His groan was tortured. His hands flexed in her hair, pulling slightly, while his flesh twitched in her hand and mouth. She saw his abdomen tighten and his whole body seemed to shake.

She would have smiled, but she wanted to keep pleasuring him. She anointed and used her tongue to search out the spots that made him curse and gasp, then bobbed her head a little, experimenting.

With a tortured noise, he used his grip on her hair to pull himself free of the suction of her lips and unsteadily petted down the back of her head, then under her jaw, forcing her to look up at him.

"Another time I'll let you finish me like that," he said in a voice that was graveled and carnal. "I'll look forward to it." His thumb scraped across her bottom lip. "But I want inside you more than I've ever wanted anything in my life."

A tiny sob of helpless arousal throbbed in her throat. She felt too weak to finish undressing, but that was okay because he was already peeling her top off before he kicked his jeans to the floor.

Seconds later, he loomed over her, pressing her onto her back again. He braced himself on an elbow, but his other hand was free and roamed her torso in a possessive claiming, sweeping to her waist and across her stomach, then up to cup her throat. He scraped his teeth against her chin.

"I want you in ways that aren't civilized. Stop me if you get scared."

"I won't." She trusted him. She always had.

His mouth twisted with a hint of cynicism, as though he knew more than she did, but he pressed his lips to her collarbone while his scorching touch went down her front again, pausing to squeeze her hip before searing the top of her thigh.

"Do you want me to wear a condom?" He caught her earlobe between his lips and gently sucked.

Did she want his baby? Her mother's cautions rang briefly through her mind. She ought to heed them, she knew. They weren't married yet, and there was that small anxious part of her that worried something would happen and he would decide he didn't want her, after all.

But when she checked in with her heart, and the part of her that yearned to be a mother, she not only wanted children, she wanted him to be their father.

"Oh…only if you want to," she said tentatively.

He lifted his head long enough to look into her eyes, doing that thing where his near-black eyes swallowed her soul, leaving her trembling.

She closed her eyes and tried to bring his mouth to hers, wanting the mindlessness again. She rolled toward him, seeking the delicious brush of his naked skin with her own, but he wanted her on her back. He pressed her flat and she let him settle between her legs. Eloise set light hands on his shoulders, wanting this, but suffering last-minute apprehension as the reality closed in on her. He was an imposing presence, tense and strong and so casual with his propriety touch. So *strong*.

He was so attuned to her, however, that he lifted his mouth from nuzzling the corner of hers and asked gruffly, "Second thoughts?"

"Nervous," she admitted, and skated her hands across the bulk of his shoulders.

"You didn't seem nervous a few minutes ago. You seemed to know exactly what you were doing."

She smiled with bashful pleasure and sifted her fingers into his hair, encouraging him to linger so they could kiss more deeply.

As they did, all the small sparks of nerves inside her began to pulse with renewed longing. She grew melty and soft and moved her legs against his, reveling in the textures and flex of his muscles.

"You're very beautiful." He only spoke Greek to her now and it felt even more intimate and sincere to hear him say these things in his native tongue. "You know that, don't you?"

She didn't. She wasn't voluptuous or stately or glamorous, but she felt very sensuous as his mouth sought under her chin. She arched her neck, luxuriating in the damp kisses he left on her throat.

"And here," he murmured, cupping her modest breast and sliding down to roll her nipple with his tongue.

"You're not disappointed that—? *Oh*." Sharp sensations lanced into her belly and lower, flooding her loins with renewed heat. With urgency.

"That you prefer to go braless? How could I be disappointed in that?"

"I didn't think you noticed."

He paused in moving from one nipple to the other. "I

always notice, *asteri mou*. It turns me on." He closed his mouth over the tip of her other breast, curling her toes.

She writhed, fingers in his hair, body feeling not her own.

When his open-mouthed kisses trailed down her abdomen, she shifted her legs, conflicted. She wanted that. Loved it. But…

"I thought you wanted…"

To be inside me.

"What I want, *ómorfi mou*, is for you to want me as badly as I want you. Open your legs and let me remind you how good I can make you feel. Yes…" His breath hissed in pleasure while his wide shoulders nudged her thighs.

He did make her feel incredible. She didn't bother with false modesty or biting back the moans he elicited from her. She let herself sink into the hot pool of wanton sensuality, giving herself over to him completely.

But just when she was nearing the peak, when she was growing blind with need, he moved his mouth to her inner thigh.

"What—?" She picked up her head, almost frantic. Did she do something wrong?

"Now you know." His teeth scraped her thigh before he closed his lips against her leg and applied light suction, as though drawing the juice from a peach. "This is how I've felt for years." He continued to trace his thumb against her aching flesh, keeping her on the precipice while avoiding the swollen knot of nerves that begged for the brush of his touch.

She panted, ready to cry she was so aroused. His soft kisses against the crease of her thigh and her belly were sweet pinpricks of torture. Then his mouth was at her breast again, sucking so strongly she curled her nails into his shoulders with urgency.

His kiss on her mouth stole everything from her. She had no defenses left. All of her was his for the taking. Forever and always.

Which he knew because the wide dome of his sex slid against the slippery, ready flesh between her thighs.

"Tell me to stop if it hurts." He was prodding for entry.

She tossed her head, not caring if it did. There was no tension in her now. Only need.

As the pressure increased and the stretch threatened pain, she reveled in the sensation because it was him. Because this was what she wanted more than her next breath. Because he was filling her and joining with her. His hips pulsed once, twice, then slid deep enough that his pelvis was flush against hers.

She shook under the magnitude of this moment, feeling both overwhelmed and jubilant. Taken and possessed, but accepted. She was offering herself to him and he was claiming her, but she was the one holding him deep inside herself.

He was shaking with tension, she realized, and ran her hands over him because she could. His body was iron and heat and couched power, hips pinned to hers while his sex pulsed intimately inside her.

His hand cradled the side of her face. "Mine," he claimed gruffly.

She was. She turned her face enough to open her mouth over the tip of his thumb.

His body flexed in reaction. His movement sent a small quake through her abdomen.

They both groaned and, in the next second, he shifted so he could move more freely. His flesh dragged from hers only to return with more intention. More ferocity and depth.

He dropped his fist to the blanket beside her ear and she brought her knees up to bracket his ribs.

"Tell me—" He swore, teeth gritted. "Tell me if I'm too rough."

"Don't stop," she cried because the friction had shot her straight back to the pinnacle and, impossibly, she was soaring past it. Higher.

Her whole body was one raw, erotic nerve. Her senses were overloaded by their combined scent and the damp brush of skin on skin. They were both breathing raggedly, releasing tight agonized noises. The bed was shaking as he moved with more speed and power. She couldn't see. Her eyes were closed or she'd gone blind. She didn't care. Her loins burned in the most exquisite way while his movements pushed her to the absolute edge of her endurance.

Then, for one eternal second, she felt nothing. She left this earthly existence and saw the wide expanse of heaven open before her, then she slammed back into a body that was pummeled by such waves of intense sexual pleasure she clung to him and screamed.

His hips crashed into hers again and again before he held himself deep inside her, arms straight as he released his own shout of exalted defeat.

Konstantin managed to roll off her and drag her close so she wouldn't smother or chill, but that was all he had in him. His muscles were twitching as though he'd finished a marathon. He was still catching his breath and waiting for his heart rate to slow.

He couldn't even open his eyes so his brain should have flatlined into unconsciousness, but his mind was racing like he'd hit a mental iceberg.

This was what he'd been afraid of. This depth of want. This need to make an irrevocable claim.

Until this moment, he had avoided articulating to himself why Eloise seemed so dangerous to him, but now he knew. The gratification of having her in his life, in his arms, in his bed put him in that horrible state of treasuring something that could be taken from him.

Why couldn't it have just been a desire for sex? His libido was something that could be satisfied by his own fist, if necessary. Or any woman. He met willing partners all the time. He preferred to want things he could find in quantity or provide for himself. That's why he stockpiled money and houses and estates that grew food. So he would never be without those things.

He didn't allow himself to want abstract things that were impossible to truly own, like one specific woman. He didn't want to have this pulse beat inside him that said, *This one. Only this one will do.*

Nevertheless, as she shifted and a tendril of her hair slid in a tickling ribbon against his knuckle, he turned his wrist so he could play with the fine strands, smug in his right to do so.

The alarm bells continued clanging inside him. He was sexually satisfied, yes, but there was a greedier beast in him that wasn't yet calm. He had told himself he was marrying her to ease his sense of obligation to Ilias and expose Antoine, but he was marrying Eloise because he wanted to keep her in his life and protect her. He wanted to tend her like a fire, to keep her glowing bright.

He wanted to get her pregnant, apparently, because they'd had sex without protection. He should damned well have thought that through more carefully, but in his most primal of lizard brains, he wanted to have sex again and again until he knew they were bound inextricably by a child. Children.

He couldn't even fathom what that would look like. But he wanted it. Which made it yet another thing he was deeply wary of reaching for.

With a sensuous little sound, she rolled herself half atop him and set her chin on her hand. Her breasts flattened against his ribs and her heavy eyelids blinked as though she were waking from a spell. Her lips were soft and still pouted from their kisses. Her sigh was one of supreme contentment.

"If I run a bath, will you join me?"

Retreat, he told himself.

He ought to offer to run it in her room and encourage her to sleep in her own bed, but his finger swept her hair off her cheek and tucked it behind her ear.

"I'll bring the wine."

CHAPTER THIRTEEN

NEMO WENT TO Athens to spend Christmas with his family, but Eloise and Konstantin weren't alone on Christmas Eve. Filomena asked if her children could come caroling. She had two boys and a girl and the older two each brought a friend.

Eloise eagerly welcomed them into the house and accompanied them on the piano, singing along with great enjoyment. She had prepared little bags of sweets that she handed out when they finished up. Then Konstantin made their eyes nearly pop out of their heads by giving them envelopes stuffed with a hundred euros each.

"*Kýrie*," Filomena protested, but Eloise assured her she was wasting her breath. If she had learned nothing else about Konstantin, she now knew him to be a ridiculously generous man behind that facade of stony aloofness.

Later, they attended a casual neighborhood party and came home to make love and sleep late.

On Christmas morning, Eloise woke and stretched against her fiancé's solid heat. She reveled in waking naked against him, thinking that in this moment, her life was as perfect as it could get.

Except for that tiny thread of doubt that continued to run through her, the one that said this was too perfect. Too easy.

She wanted to believe that time would prove her wrong. Eventually, she would trust in this union, but in these early days, she couldn't seem to keep from feeling quietly anxious that she was kidding herself. That this would all disappear in a blink of an eye.

Which meant she ought to embrace what she had while she had it, literally.

The brush of their skin was pure decadence, as was the right to reach across and caress his back and buttocks. She gave in to the urge to ease atop him and drape herself over his back.

"I feel the weight of expectation," he said into his pillow. "You want to go downstairs to see what's under the tree, don't you?"

"I want to see if you like my gift."

His back rose and fell beneath her in a sigh.

Why was he so resistant to gifts?

She turned her lips against his satiny skin and kissed his spine, then moved in a whole-body caress. The plane between his shoulder blades felt each side of her face as she stropped like a cat leaving its scent. She shifted higher to kiss the back of his neck. Her breasts swayed against the plane of his back and the hard curve of his backside was caressed by her stomach and the graze of her mound. She bracketed his hip with her knee and slid her arms beneath the pillow alongside his.

"If you'd rather stay in bed a few more minutes, I could be persuaded," she said.

He rolled so he was on his back and she could straddle his hips.

Afterward, they showered, then bumped their way downstairs, drunk on sex and each other.

Filomena was spending the day with her family so Eloise started the coffee and put the casserole that Filomena had prepared into the oven. It was loaded with peppers and artichoke, herbs and sun-dried tomatoes, then topped with feta cheese.

When the coffee was ready, she brought the cups into the lounge, finding Konstantin at the windows. The pile of gifts under the tree had grown by at least a half dozen.

"What have you done?" She sifted through them, able to tell from some of the wrapping that there was at least one bottle of perfume and a designer scarf.

"Open this one first." He plucked an envelope from the tree. It was tickets to a symphony performance in New York in the spring.

She pressed the envelope to her chest. "You'll come with me?"

"Unless you want to take your mother. Or someone else?"

"Mom would enjoy it, but I'll only ask her if something comes up and you can't make it. I'd rather take you. Thank you." She kissed him. "Okay, now mine." She plucked the small flat gift from beneath the tree and curled into the corner of the sofa, holding it out to him.

His expression stiffened as he came to sit beside her.

"Does it really bother you?" She held the flat shape between her pressed palms, distressed that she was causing him more discomfort than pleasure.

His cheek ticked. "It's a childish reaction," he said, mouth curling with dismay. "I was given something when I was young. It meant a lot to me and it was destroyed deliberately, to hurt me. It ruined my pleasure in receiving gifts."

"That happened at school? Sometimes girls were spiteful that way, too."

"No." His brow flexed briefly. "Things like that happened at school, yes, but I didn't care about that. I had stopped letting myself feel any sort of sentiment by then. Things are things. I can buy them for myself if I want them. I don't…" He set his hands on his knees and looked straight ahead as though searching for the words. "I don't like the sensation of someone knowing me well enough to give me something I'll like. It feels like a weakness. Like I'm painting a target on my chest."

She looked at the gift she held and chewed the corner of her mouth. "Now I'm worried this could hurt you. I was excited when I thought of it, certain you would like it, but…" She drew a breath that made her lungs ache and winced as she offered it. "If you don't want to open it, that's okay. Put it in a drawer and we never have to talk about this again."

"Well, now I'm curious. Is it anthrax?" He picked at the paper, in no hurry, but it became obvious very quickly that it was a framed photo.

He tore away the last scrap of paper and stilled with surprised recognition.

She watched his profile as he studied the photo of himself with Ilias. For a long moment, he said nothing, gave away nothing.

"Are you upset?" She set a concerned hand on his shoulder.

"No. You're right. I like it very much." His hand came up to cover hers while he tilted the frame as though looking for some hidden detail. "Did you use AI?"

"What? No! I took it."

"When?" He turned his head, expression astonished.

"The day you came to Ilias's apartment, when you were supposed to spend Christmas with us. See? That's the tree behind you, before I started to decorate it. You helped him carry it up. I made you two pose in front of it. It was my

DANI COLLINS   165

sly way of getting a photo of my secret platonic boyfriend. Secret because you didn't know," she explained. "And platonic because…"

"I knew," he said out of the side of his mouth, but the corners were tilting up as he studied it again.

In the photo, Konstantin still had his arm outstretched to hold the tree upright. Ilias had looped his arm beneath Konstantin's and set his hand on Konstantin's opposite shoulder. Her brother wore his most carefree grin, always up for a photo while Konstantin had a look of patient tolerance on his face.

"He would have beheaded me if he knew what I was thinking that day. I would have deserved it," he added with dark humor. "But thank you for this. I don't let myself think of him too often. It makes me feel robbed. And I'll forever be sorry I didn't stay longer that day. Didn't spend more time with him when I had the chance."

"I feel like that, too." She looped her arms around his neck, leaning her head against his as she also looked at the photo. "But I try to remember the laughs and be grateful he was in my life at all. Without him, I wouldn't have met you so he's still bringing good things into my life, isn't he?" It was the closest she dared get to admitting how much she was growing to love him.

Konstantin set the photo on the end table and drew her into his lap. "You're like him in that way. You always see the bright side. To me, everything ends in pain and loss."

"Because you lost your mother so young? Did you lose your father at the same time?"

His expression turned stony and she felt him withdraw so completely, it was as though his body temperature dropped several degrees. "I did."

She felt the pain he was trying to stem in the tension that had invaded his embrace.

"You don't have to tell me about it if you don't want to," she assured him, cuddling into him, trying to radiate warmth and comfort through his skin, into his heart and bones. Into his soul. "But you can."

"Not today," he said after a brief hesitation. His hand roamed over her hair and down her back, as though trying to soften his refusal. "I don't want to ruin Christmas. Get the blue one." He nudged her knee.

It was a pendant to match the earrings he'd given her in Nice, dangling from an ornate Byzantine chain.

"This is too much," she scolded. "I'm going to absolutely smother you in gifts next year to make up for it. Actually, when is your birthday?"

"I'll never tell."

"Nemo will."

"Not if he wants to keep his job."

"Then I'll pick a random day and call it your birthday," she warned as she straddled his lap, pleased that her frothy skirt allowed it.

The confection of white feathers piled around her like a snowdrift and he dug his hands into the folds to bracket her hips while she affixed the chain beneath her loose hair. She centered the stone against the wine red of the top that hugged her torso.

"Thank you," she said sincerely. "It's very pretty."

"So are you."

She loved seeing his expression relaxed like this. His gaze leisurely caressed her braless breasts—yes, she had forgone a bra for him. It meant her nipples were constantly stimulated by the soft knit, standing at subtle attention and now prickling and tightening that little bit more as he admired her.

It was such a perfect moment that she almost said it. Almost admitted she loved him. It wasn't the immature crush of her teen years or infatuation with an idea of a man. It wasn't the beguilement of being showered with gifts, either.

She was beginning to know him, truly know him. He was withdrawn, yes, but beneath that hardened veneer was a man who had a chewy caramel center. He was outrageously generous—in bed and elsewhere. He kept his promises and he made her feel special and sexy and cherished. If he hadn't been able to afford a sapphire, he would have found another way to make her feel as though she was incredibly important to him, of that she had no doubt.

He was important to her. Did he know that?

Sliding her fingers into his hair, she leaned forward and set her mouth to his, trying to make him feel the love that was brimming out of her. She didn't know what the hidden sadness in him was, or what made him cynical or who had deliberately hurt him, but she wanted to heal all of that. The only way she knew to do it was to love him. To pour her feelings over him and dispel all his inner shadows with the golden light that glowed from the depths of her heart.

His breath hissed in and his fingertips bit through the downy skirt. She thought for a moment that he was going to move her off him, as though she was touching some part of him that was too raw.

Then a groan rattled deep in his chest. His hands found her breasts through the cashmere and his thumbs stroked against her nipples.

It was good, so good, but also a tiny bit painful. Not physically. It was painful to love him this much and not know how he felt about her. She wanted to tell him how she felt, but feared he would push her away if she did.

So she showed him. She burrowed her hand beneath her skirt and found his fly.

He bunched her skirt up and out of the way, then ran his finger beneath the placket of the tanga she wore. When she was stroking his steely erection, he moved the silk aside and helped her guide his tip to her entrance.

With a small shudder, she sank upon him. The anxiety of not being able to fully reach him dissipated when they were like this—not just joined physically, but connected on a deeper level. When he caressed her, he seemed to know where and how she needed it. When she pressed her mouth to his, their kiss ebbed and flowed between sweet and passionate, inciting and easing, then inflaming again.

They had made love only a couple of hours ago, much like this, so it shouldn't have felt this urgent. At first, it was simply pleasure and desire building at its own pace. They barely moved as they sought skin and ran their mouths into each other's necks and exchanged wordless praise and appreciation.

But for some reason his talk of things ending in pain and loss played in her ears like a ticking clock. She didn't want him to be right. She wanted them fused indelibly for the rest of their lives. She began to move with more purpose, as though she could forge a more permanent connection through force of will.

Her clamor seemed to ignite something similar in him. His kiss grew harder. Hungrier. His hands clamped onto her hips, urging her to take him deeper. Her breathing grew erratic and she clung to the back of the sofa as she rode him, feeling as though she raced toward a paradise that could turn out to be a mirage.

It was real, though. It had to be, because orgasm was slamming into her and his arms were folding around her, crushing her as he threw back his head and lifted his hips and shouted out her name.

Joyous pleasure cascaded through her, but so did something else. Fear.

She folded onto him and closed her eyes, suffused with bliss, but also a sense of being stalked. Of the future being uncertain and clouded and dark.

When she turned her mouth against the side of his face, his profile was grave, making her wonder if he felt that same lack of permanence, too.

They flew to Athens on the morning of the twenty-seventh.

Eloise's mother had invited them to marry in her villa on the morning of the twenty-eighth. Since it was the home Eloise had grown up in, she thought it would feel as though Ilias were with them in spirit. Konstantin said he was happy to indulge her and her mother.

Lilja had been texting a lot more than normal, seeming to have reclaimed her phone for wedding plans. She was determined to make Eloise's day as special as possible and was fussing over every decision from flowers to music, from wedding breakfast to photo sitting. She even wanted Eloise's approval on her mother-of-the-bride dress.

Antoine was still managing to be a pain, though, now putting all his energy into stonewalling Konstantin.

"I haven't even asked him for the audit I want," Konstantin said with disgust. "He refuses to give my team contact info for his lawyers and accountants. Their request for a list of assets that belong to you, to include in our prenup, is being ignored altogether."

"Because there aren't any," Eloise pointed out.

"Then he should say that, shouldn't he?" Konstantin was no longer the lover she'd been pre-honeymooning with on Crete. He was crisp-voiced and hardened as he changed into a suit of charcoal armor.

"I was thinking of booking a massage after my fitting." She'd had a limited selection for wedding outfits since she was marrying so quickly, but Ghaliya had found her an elegant skirt suit that only needed a tuck and hemming. The seamstress would be here soon. "I could ask for a his-and-hers session this afternoon?"

"No. I hate people touching me."

She blinked, shocked as much by his blunt, vehement tone as the words.

He checked himself and a curl of irony arrived on the line of his stern mouth.

"I mean strangers, obviously. I'm addicted to your touch." He came across to set a hand on her hip and drop a tender kiss on her mouth. "I have meetings with Nemo all day, anyway. Book something for yourself if you want to."

"Maybe I can talk Mom into joining me at a spa for a few hours. I don't know how else to pry Antoine away from her." He was like a lamprey.

"I'll send the car back so it's here for you if you decide to go out."

"Thank you."

Konstantin left and Eloise sighed in loss, finding this return to reality very jarring. Life was so much simpler when they made love, then made coffee. He worked off his laptop while she played piano. Maybe they walked after lunch or drove around the island before returning home to make love again. It had been bliss.

It had been impossible to have doubts about their future

when she was with him all the time, drinking in his attention and affection.

She called her mother and wasn't surprised when the call was not picked up. She texted her an invitation to the spa and received a reply that had to be from Antoine.

Going to the bank today.

To get the ring from Petros? Eloise wondered. She could only imagine how that was sitting with Antoine.

Purely to let him know she wasn't fooled, she texted back.

Are you taking her or are you meeting with Konstantin?

He left her on Read, the jerk. He probably deleted it on that end, too, so her mother wouldn't see it. Eloise had lost her ability to give him the benefit of the doubt and was starting to think she would have to have a more serious chat with her mother.

What a dreadful thought. She'd wait until the wedding was out of the way, she decided. Not only would her mother have that happy memory, but Eloise would feel more secure in her own position and ability to support her.

The seamstress arrived and Eloise was tied up for the next hour. She was about to settle in for a relaxing hour of playing piano when Konstantin called to snap, "The car is waiting downstairs for you. I need you to meet me at your mother's."

"Is she okay? I thought Antoine was taking her to the bank."

"They're going to the *bank*? When? Which one?" He swore and told someone to, "Get that notice to all of those institutions. Immediately. I'm sure your mother is fine," he told Eloise, but his voice was steely and cold. "I'll find out where they're going and have the car bring you to me there. Leave as soon as you can."

"O—" he'd already hung up "—kay."

What on earth had he found out?

CHAPTER FOURTEEN

KONSTANTIN'S INNER WARRIOR was already agitated. Seeing Eloise enter the lobby of the bank only riled his inner protector more. He wanted to shout and clatter his shield in warning against anyone who might dare to threaten her.

He wanted to kill the man who had.

Despite her worried expression, Eloise was her beautiful self. Her dark hair bounced in waves that framed her face as she moved with purpose toward him, looking confident in her double-breasted coatdress over heeled boots.

She had blossomed in this short time with him, not only reverting to the cheeky young woman he'd known in the past, but growing past her into a sophisticated woman who made his insides twist with admiration and pride.

In this moment, however, all he could see was the thin ill-fitting elf suit she'd been wearing when she'd been scraping by in New York—thanks to Antoine's machinations.

"The manager put them in a VIP lounge next to the vault," Konstantin said, nodding curtly at their escort to take them there.

"What happened?" she asked in the elevator.

"I finally spoke to Cyrus. He's standing by to talk with your mother." He slid a look to the bank employee, reluctant to elaborate until they had privacy. "It won't fall to you to tell her."

"Tell her what?" Her eyes widened in alarm, but the doors opened. They were escorted down a carpeted hall, through an open cage door, and into another anteroom where Antoine and her mother were sipping coffee.

"Darling!" Lilja stood, smiling with surprised pleasure as she stepped forward to hug Eloise. "What are you doing here? You're not putting my ring directly into your own box. No. It hasn't seen the sun in years. I want you to *wear* it."

"Actually…um… I'm not sure why we're here?" Eloise looked to Konstantin.

"Neither am I," Antoine said with cold precision, holding Konstantin's hate-filled glare with a staggering amount of audacity.

My fault, Konstantin realized with a fresh kick of guilt.

His neglect of these two women had allowed Antoine to believe he could not only get away with what he'd done, but that he still might.

"I apologize for the delay, Madame Roussea." The bank manager entered. He dismissed the other employee with a nod, then addressed Lilja. "I've had an urgent call from our head of security. He's requesting you thoroughly examine the contents of your safety deposit box while you're here to ensure the inventory is exactly as you expect it to be."

"Goodness…" Lilja touched her collar and looked at all of them in turn. "Has there been a robbery?"

"No," the manager assured with a calming smile. "Our hope is that this is a false alarm. Will you come with me, please?"

Antoine was sending daggers into Konstantin from his narrowed eyes. Eloise looked as apprehensive as her mother. The room was filled with a charged silence.

"Take your time," Konstantin said to Lilja, finding as calm a tone as he could. "We'll stay here with Antoine. I need to speak with him, anyway."

Still faltering with confusion, Lilja followed the bank manager out.

Konstantin pressed the door closed and pinned the older man with his contemptuous glare.

"I suppose you think you've gained the upper hand in some way?" Antoine sneered.

"Not me, no. My fiancée is the one with all the power here. Even more when she turns twenty-five and is entitled to become cotrustee of Lilja's fortune."

"I didn't want to believe he was that rotten." Eloise grappled for the back of the nearest chair.

Konstantin took a quick step to grasp under her elbow, bracing her.

"Until then, you only have the privilege of consultation and the right to demand a full audit if you feel there is just cause," he explained. "I would say there's more than just cause, seeing as Antoine has been withholding your living allowance and all the statements and notifications that you ought to be receiving."

"Is that why you wanted to marry me off to Edoardo?" she asked Antoine with outrage.

"Now you know why *he* wants to marry you," Antoine scoffed, pointing at Konstantin.

"Nice try," Konstantin snorted, but was aware of his hand tightening incrementally on Eloise's arm, feeling under threat at a very primeval level. "I only found out about this today. Cyrus was surprised you didn't know about these arrangements," he continued explaining to Eloise. "He sent a letter to you at your mother's home when he retired, outlining everything in detail. I'm guessing it was waylaid." Konstantin curled his lip with disgust as he looked to the reason for the letter going astray.

Antoine was stiff and watchful, mouth twitching into a snarl.

"She wasn't even coming home," Antoine said as though it was a sensible defense of his actions. "She was behaving as erratically as a drug addict. I was protecting Lilja's fortune from someone who was not responsible enough to use that money wisely. Now she's marrying *you*? How well do you think that will play in court?"

Antoine's derisive tone was a poison-tipped arrow directly into Konstantin's chest. He shouldn't have been surprised. This particular secret reared its head occasionally, but it always leaked toxins throughout his whole body, turning it to stone. He only wished he'd taken his chance when he'd had it. Eloise had asked him a few days ago, and he'd turned away from the opportunity to bare all. He hadn't wanted to ruin the day.

Instead, it would ruin her view of him.

He had the old sense of holding something he had desperately wanted and having it snatched from his grasp. Again.

"I do my homework, too." Antoine's mouth wore a smile that was nothing but a denigrating stretch of his lips. It sent a chill of premonition through Eloise's nerves, curdling her breakfast in her stomach.

"See if your mother—" Konstantin began, but Antoine spoke over him in a tone of evil satisfaction.

"His father murdered his mother. Has he told you that?"

Eloise had started to obey the nudge of Konstantin's hand.

Antoine's shocking statement was so cold and unex-

pected, so gratingly harsh while delivered so conversation-
ally, she felt as though she'd been struck. Her ears buzzed
and her skin turned to ice.

She turned back to see Konstantin retreating into the
furthest depths of himself, presenting only a granite shell
and the radiation of hatred directed toward her stepfather.

The crackle of danger between the men had her flight-
or-fight response activating, sending stinging adrenaline
through her limbs.

"He died in prison. Violently." Antoine continued to
turn the knife. "It was all covered up by his grandfather,
but that's where he comes from. Do you really want to tie
yourself to a man like that? Is that the kind of man you
want to *sleep* next to?"

Konstantin's hands had been all over her for days, but
that wasn't why Eloise felt so sick right now. No, it was the
vileness of Antoine dragging up something so painful and
leaving it like entrails in the middle of the floor.

"You think you're the first to throw that in my face?"
Konstantin said with icy disdain. "Or that it gives you any
leverage over me? Eloise is the one with the power right
now. Cyrus has already sworn a statement. My lawyers are
sending notices recommending all of Lilja's accounts be
frozen until the appropriate trustee is identified. If you've
been squirreling funds to other accounts, it will come to
light."

"And you'll do what?" Antoine spat in her direction.
"You can't charge her husband with stealing from their
common property. She was of sound mind when she put
me in charge. You have nothing and you'll get nothing. All
you'll do is break her heart."

She would. Eloise knew from experience how awful this
would become and was already sick as she absorbed that

she would have to do it again. It killed her that she would
have to shatter what peace and comfort her mother had
managed to find these last years, but she was seeing that it
was a horrible illusion, anyway.

"I'm going to tell her that you don't deserve her because
you don't."

Antoine puffed up and Konstantin stepped between
them.

The door opened behind them and her mother came in,
still flustered.

"Everything was fine," she said with a shaken smile.
"I'm not sure what the fuss was about. The manager said
he would be in touch soon with more information. What,
um… Is everything all right?" She flicked her gaze around
the room. The worried lines in her expression etched themselves deeper.

"*Parfait*," Antoine lied smoothly. "We've come to a gentleman's agreement. I told you lawyers weren't necessary.
Shall we go?"

"Not yet. I have to give Eloise the ring. Look at it." Her
mother smiled mistily as she showed the platinum set diamond on her hand. "I forgot how much I loved it."

"Keep it on, Mom. I'm taking you home." Eloise's voice
shook as hard as the rest of her. Everything within her
wanted to run from this moment. She had hoped to never
go through it again, but… "Antoine isn't coming. He's not
the man you think he is."

"They're not marrying," Antoine blurted with a cruel
bare of his teeth. "Once you hear why, you'll question all
of this."

Eloise opened her mouth, appalled he would use Konstantin's past as a weapon.

Before she could protest that learning about Konstantin's past didn't change her view of him, Konstantin spoke.

"We don't need to marry. Not anymore. Not when Eloise has money and power of her own."

His blunt words landed straight in the middle of her heart, shattering it like glass.

"I'll keep him here," Konstantin said in her direction, without actually looking at her. "He can either give me a list of the relevant accounts and assets, or he can give them to the police. I have all the time in the world for him to make that decision."

"What on earth? Eloise, tell me that...?" Lilja looked with agonized eyes from her husband to Konstantin's grim expression to Eloise.

Regret rose to choke her voice as Eloise said, "I'm sorry, Mom. Let's go home and talk. We'll call Cyrus and he'll explain." As she nudged her mother out the door in front of her, she told Antoine, "Your suitcases will be on the stoop in an hour. Don't come into the house."

Konstantin entered the villa he'd only been in a handful of times. He and Ilias had both lived in Athens when not at school, but Konstantin wasn't a social person. He had sent regrets to all the parties Ilias had invited him to through their early years. Later, Ilias had been in the US, so they had met for the odd sporting event or a beer if Konstantin happened to be there.

No, the last time he'd been here was immediately after Ilias was laid to rest. Konstantin had stood on the periphery while people ate finger food and made small talk. Eloise had looked a lot like she did now—as though the life force had been drained out of her.

That was his fault. He didn't regret telling her the truth

about Antoine, but he would always regret that she had had to hear about his parents the way she had.

"Mom's lying down," she said, hugging herself as she met him in the parlor. "She's upset, obviously. I should have told her that Antoine had left me stuck in New York, but..." She rubbed her brow. "He had her convinced that I was growing up and leaving the nest so she didn't question it too much. Cyrus has encouraged us to pursue a proper investigation, but he doubts there'll be much fallout for Antoine beyond embarrassment, since Mom was in her right mind when she gave him control."

"I should have checked on you both a lot sooner. That will always sit on my conscience."

"Don't—I don't want to be anything on your conscience, Konstantin. I would hope I'm more than a duty or obligation to you by now?" Her brow pleated as she searched his expression.

He looked away, unable to express what she was to him because he could already feel that fragile connection between them thinning and fraying.

"The wedding is off." He stated it first, because he knew it to be true. He had known it when Antoine brought up his past.

Agonized helplessness flashed across her expression, but she didn't contradict him.

"Mom's a wreck and she's literally the only person I would want there. She'll need me for a while. Then I have this Gordian knot to untangle." She waved at the imaginary mountain of paperwork. "But that doesn't mean I don't want to marry you."

"This all happened very quickly." Ten days. He hadn't even been allotted his full twelve days. That was par for the course for him so he brushed aside how cheated he felt.

"Don't." She took a few faltering steps toward him. "Don't act like I was caught up in the moment. *I love you*, Konstantin. I've always loved you. You know that. I was hoping you were starting to love me, too."

He drew a breath that felt laced with arsenic. "You told me a few days ago that you had spent years idolizing someone who doesn't exist. What you're feeling is sexual desire and nostalgia and gratitude. It's not really love, Eloise."

"That's a horrible thing to say to someone. Do you realize that?" She moved so she was in his line of sight, but not close enough to touch. Her chin set with belligerence and her fists knotted at her sides. "Have your feelings toward me been equally superficial? Were you horny and mildly entertained and now you're bored so you're cutting things short?"

She was right. They were stooping to saying horrible things.

"Our marrying is one of those things that looks like it will work, but it never would have. I know what you want, Eloise. You want me to be emotionally accessible and I'm *not*. I would hurt you in the long run so let's end it now while the damage is minimal."

"How would you hurt me? You're not…violent." She swallowed the last word.

"No." Although he'd had a moment there with Antoine when he could have happily pushed him out a window. "And I'll do my best to quash it if Antoine tries to take my story to the press. I've done it before, but the day will come when it gets out. It's not something you want to be married to. You don't want it overshadowing your mother, either."

"Was that what you didn't want to tell me at Christmas?" she asked with such gentle care that his heart contracted.

"Yes." And he didn't want to tell her now, but he would

give her the bones of it. "My father was not unlike Antoine, capable of charm to hide the fact he was a monster. My mother kept seeing him even after my grandfather expressly forbade it. When she got pregnant, they married and my father moved us to an isolated farm. He had violent outbursts that grew worse over time. She tried to leave, asked my grandfather for help, but he refused. He told her she'd made her bed."

"That's awful." She rubbed her chest.

"Yes. One day, he caught us trying to leave and really went after her. I got in the way and he knocked me across the cottage. I don't remember anything afterward except waking in the hospital to the news my mother was dead. My grandfather came to get me. I never saw my father again."

"Konstantin—"

He held up a hand to ward her off. "I'm not telling you this for sympathy, Eloise. I want you to understand why... God." He pinched the bridge of his nose. "I don't want to look back or talk about it or *build new memories* because those things don't *last*. I don't want to learn to care about someone only to have him crash his damned airplane. I don't want to fall in love with someone—" he pointed accusingly at her "—and have her taken from me."

"Nobody is taking me. You're pushing me away."

"I'm taking control of the inevitable."

"You don't know it's inevitable. You're making it happen so you can prove to yourself that you're right." Her mouth quivered as she removed her ring and offered it. "But I won't force you to stay in a relationship you don't want. I've always known my love for you was unrequited. I won't keep fooling myself that you'll come around. At least I tried. I'll be able to move on now. Thank you for helping us. We'll be okay now."

Would they? He wouldn't.

"That's yours." He ignored the ring and walked out, heart on a pike. He was so nauseated he nearly threw up in the car.

CHAPTER FIFTEEN

AFTER A NIGHT where Eloise and her mother both spent hours crying out their broken hearts, Nemo turned up.

"I know the wedding is off," he said when Eloise started to cry. "No, *kyría*, I'm here with a press release. Can you review it, please?"

Konstantin had drafted a statement that the wedding had been postponed due to a family concern. Since that was followed almost immediately by a statement that Lilja was divorcing Antoine, the gossip around the canceled nuptials was minimal.

Nemo then stuck around to speak with Cyrus and assist with revoking Antoine's rights to the trust. He made phone calls and canceled bank accounts and issued notices to expel Antoine from all of Lilja's properties—including the house in Nice. Technically, they both owned that one, but it was now a contested asset in their divorce proceedings. Nemo also found her mother a good lawyer for that.

"We're monopolizing you," Eloise said when he continued to turn up even after they'd rung in the New Year. "Doesn't Konstantin need you?"

"One of my colleagues has taken over my position. Since I was familiar with your situation, I'm to assist you until you no longer need assistance. Also, because your accounts have been frozen until the audits can be conducted, *Kýrie* Galanis will cover your legal fees and any other expenses while you wait for access to your funds to be granted."

Of course, he would. She stifled a sigh of despair, angry with him for looking after them so well, but from a distance. Was he afraid to *accept* her love? Was that it? Had she smothered him? Or not given enough?

After so many years of fantasy, then having marriage to him within her grasp, she struggled to let go of the dream. She lay awake at night wishing she'd done this or that differently, but the reality was he didn't want to marry her. She had to accept that.

She only wished it didn't hurt *so much*.

"Did your tea go cold while you were speaking to your friend?" Nemo asked her mother. Lilja was making a face over the cup she'd just picked up. "Let me ask the kitchen to make you a fresh one."

"Thank you, Nemo." She handed over cup and saucer. "I have no idea how we would manage if you weren't here with us. I think poor Konstantin has lost himself an assistant."

Eloise choked on a small astonished laugh, her first shred of humor in a week. How had she and Ilias never realized their mother needed a male assistant?

Thankfully, Eloise was kept busy meeting with all the lawyers and accountants, hiring a cotrustee who would teach her the ropes of managing so much money, and realizing that she actually had a crap ton of allowance owed to her that needed investing. It was daunting, but she was glad to be distracted.

She was so distracted, in fact, that she didn't realize her period was late until she was two weeks overdue.

A visit to the doctor confirmed her pregnancy. She sat in the exam room for a good thirty minutes afterward, crying happy-sad tears. Her first instinct was to go directly to Konstantin and tell him, but she knew what would happen. He would feel obligated to marry her and she didn't want to put him in that position. She didn't want him to propose to her again for any reason except that he had fallen in love with her.

Ugh. She was still doing it: hoping.

She would have to tell him about the baby at some point, though. The prevailing advice was to wait twelve weeks before sharing this news. She didn't want him to get attached to this pregnancy, then suffer the loss if something happened—which was a very convenient rationalization for being a coward, she knew. But she didn't know if she could face him yet without falling apart. She missed him to the point that she ached from the moment she woke to the moment she slipped into unconsciousness. Then she cried in her sleep, missing him in her dreams.

She would never resist seeing him if she stayed in Athens. She'd only lasted this long because she remembered he'd had business in Singapore in January. Once he returned, the temptation to go to him would be overpowering.

"Mom, what do you think of a change in scenery?" she asked when she returned from the doctor. "I was thinking of applying to that music therapy program again."

"In New York? Well, yes, I've always wanted to spend more than a week or two there. What about Nemo? Can he accompany us?"

Nemo was delighted by the opportunity to spend an indefinite time in the Big Apple. His boyfriend was equally excited and planned to follow as soon as he worked out some wrinkles in his own professional life.

Within a week, they were in a leased Gramercy apartment with four bedrooms, a private terrace, daily house-keeping and an attached studio apartment for Nemo.

Eloise was accepted into the program, thanks to her previous audition, but more because money talked and she now had an abundance of it. Along with starting school, she quietly took her prenatal vitamins and found a midwife, still keeping her pregnancy to herself. She was dying to tell her mother, but she wanted to tell Konstantin first.

The longer she left it, the more daunting that prospect became. She wanted a full plan in place when she told him, one that allowed her to raise the baby alone, but still provided him as much access as he wanted. It would be pure torture to see him on what she suspected would be a daily basis, but somehow they would have to make it work.

The churn of anticipation and dread drove her to the piano every day where she poured out her turmoil of joy and longing, her anguish and all the love that refused to be doused.

In fact, her feelings for him grew a little more each day, just like their baby.

Konstantin tried to retreat into the skin of numbness he'd worn most of his life, but it was shredded beyond repair. His feelings for Eloise were too sharp. Too jagged and hot and extreme.

God, he missed her. How had she become such an integral part of his life in such a short time? It wasn't just the sex. That had been mind-altering, setting a bar that he doubted would ever be reached with anyone else, but he wasn't plagued by unmet carnal need. He was instead struck repeatedly by the emptiness of his days. Absence and meaninglessness hit him like an echo in a cavern, leaving him feeling as though he was lost in the dark, bouncing into rough granite walls.

He woke to a cold empty bed. He ate his meals alone, finding no enjoyment in whatever went into his mouth. The silence was worst of all. The cruel lack of music, the absence of laughter. He even missed her innocuous questions about whether he wanted chicken for lunch.

His meetings in Asia should have been a welcome distraction, but he resented them. He hated every minute of being so far from her, but on his return to Athens, he learned she'd gone to New York. That somehow tore a fresh hole in the fabric of his existence.

He *hated* this feeling. It was the one he'd been trying to avoid, this sense of something having been taken from him. Of having a great hole within him that couldn't be filled.

Work had always been a useful panacea, but it did little for him these day except provide him with a small satisfaction that he was creating an additional layer of security for Eloise and her mother. When he advised his lawyers the wedding was off, he told them to continue updating his will to make Eloise his beneficiary.

He left her number in his phone as his emergency contact because, if he wound up on death's doorstep, he wanted her face to be the last thing he saw. Her voice to be the last thing he heard.

Would she even turn up?

I've always known my love was unrequited. I won't keep fooling myself that you'll come around.

Had he killed whatever she might have felt for him? *Was* he creating the very reality he feared so he could face it and move past it, rather than have it hang over his head? Because he didn't think he'd ever get over her absence from his life.

He desperately wanted the reassurance he hadn't hurt her too badly, but Nemo refused to be much of a spy, saying only a circumspect, "Legal hiccups have been minimal. Things are progressing."

"But how are Eloise and Lilja coping?"

"As well as could be expected, under the circumstances. *Kýrie*? I'm not sure how to broach this. Lilja—she asked me to call her that. She's made me an offer of employment. It's been such an honor to work for you. I wouldn't want you to think I'm ungrateful…"

Konstantin tuned out the rest, letting the young man say his piece before saying, "The door remains open if things change."

They ended the call and Konstantin felt as though one more thread that joined him to Eloise had been snipped. It stung like hell.

Which was why he was so surprised when Nemo contacted him a few weeks later, asking when he might be visiting New York next. Lilja wanted to have lunch with him.

Konstantin hadn't been planning anything, but booked a trip immediately, concerned.

It was a sunny February day when he met his almost mother-in-law at a restaurant located one hundred stories in the air, overlooking the city and the Hudson River.

"Lilja." He was startled to feel such an intense rush of warmth when he saw her, as though he'd missed her when, much as he liked and respected her, he didn't know her well. He didn't have any reason to feel attached to her, except through her children. "How are you?"

"I'm well. You?" Her eyes, so much like Eloise's, searched his, making him feel transparent.

"Fine," he insisted briskly. "How is Eloise?" he asked

once they were seated. "I was concerned that you wanted to see me."

"She's not ill or injured, if that's what you're asking, but she is the reason I wanted to see you."

"You're worried about her?" he guessed, suffering a stab of guilt. He had hurt her. He knew he had.

"Only insofar as any mother would be worried when she realizes her daughter has stopped drinking and turns green at the smell of bacon. I couldn't stand the stuff myself when I was carrying her."

"She's pregnant?" He nearly fell out of his chair.

"I'm assuming so. Thank you." She accepted her mimosa as it was delivered.

He drained the scotch that was set in front of him. The alcohol burned all the way into the back of his skull and down into his chest.

"Why hasn't she told me?" It was the most intense rejection, the worst kick in the teeth, he could have imagined.

I'll be able to move on now, she'd said.

Apparently, she'd meant it.

"You tell me." She looked to the diamond on her hand. It was the one from the bank, now worn in place of the rings that Antoine had given her. "I thought she had with you what I had with Petros. He was the love of my life." She sighed wistfully.

Konstantin signaled for another drink, then looked out the window, wondering if she had requested this meeting specifically to torture him.

"I'm deeply sorry that Antoine brought up your parents, Konstantin. When I realized afterward that that was what he was referring to, when he threatened you at the bank, I was sickened."

His stomach heaved and a clammy sweat rose on his skin. "Eloise told you?"

"No. She only said Antoine had threatened to expose something private that you don't like to talk about, but I was living in Greece with a son your age when it happened," she reminded him gently. "Word got around and for me, it struck close to home. I came from a troubled family, too. One I don't like to revisit, either."

His second drink arrived and he ignored it in favor of reaching out to squeeze Lilja's hand, hating to think of this delicate, infinitely kind, beautiful woman being at the hands of someone cruel.

She held onto his fingers tightly while a smile touched her mouth. Then she released him to sip her mimosa, blinking and drawing a slow breath, as though gathering her composure.

"I don't know if you ever told Ilias about any of it. I never said anything to him about you, but he said to me early in your friendship that you were the only boy at school who knew what it felt like to lose a parent and not have a father. It gave me some comfort that you had each other." Her brow flexed with poignancy. "I didn't know what to do with him back then. Losing Petros was devastating for both of us, but Ilias was so determined to grow up and take his father's place. I know I leaned on him too heavily, but when I didn't ask his advice, he was annoyed. There was no winning."

"He did insist on looking after people, whether they asked for help or not," Konstantin recalled with rueful affection.

"Didn't he?" She brightened, then grew misty. "That was Petros coming out in him. I used to wish Petros had lived to meet Eloise, so he could see what a protector Ilias turned into around her. Silly, right? If Petros had lived, I wouldn't have had her. That would be a crime because she's been such a bright light in my life. Effervescent and cuddly, spilling her love and life and music all over the place. I spoiled her. I know I did. I wanted so badly to keep her…" she cupped her hands into a tiny sheltering dome "…protected. Unstruck by life. But that's not possible."

Her elbow went onto the table and she tucked her chin into her hand, looking out the window.

"It's not," he agreed gravely. "And God, Lilja. You've had so many blows yourself. How do you carry on and remain so hopeful, knowing you could lose everything at any time? When you have lost so much?"

"Do you refuse to listen to a song because you know it will come to an end?" she asked with a wry smile and sad eyes. "Even the Parthenon will eventually be nothing but dust. You have to enjoy something while you're able *because* it's temporary. And yes, sometimes you might make a mistake and fall for the wrong person." Her mouth pursed with heartbreak and consternation. "I've done more than my share of that. I want to believe the best in people. I want to feel *loved*. Eloise has borne the brunt of my poor judgment too many times. It doesn't occur to me that anyone would hurt her, though. Why would they want to?" Her brow pleated with incomprehension. "She's so easy to love."

"She is." The words vibrated from behind his sternum, more a feeling than actual words, but they refused to be kept inside him any longer.

"Then why are you hurting her, Konstantin?" she asked with distress. "Why aren't you loving her while you have the chance?"

The whole building disappeared from beneath him and he felt himself plummeting to the ground.

He didn't have an answer. In fact, he didn't know why he was hurting himself.

* * *

Eloise's assignment was to learn and perform a song for her class that expressed an emotional conflict in her life.

She didn't know whether she would go through with playing this. Her classmates seemed nice, but they were still strangers. Did she really want to bare her soul to them? It was the point to feel vulnerable, she knew, but this was still so raw.

At least for the moment, this was only for her. She was alone in Music Room Two, begging the piano keys to tell her how to mend a broken heart.

She hummed through the lyrics about stopping the sun from shining and the rain from falling, then let herself be swept into the sweet, poignant, "La, la, la, la, la, la…"

The next lyrics were too painful to sing. She slipped back into humming for the final plea for help mending her heart and learning to live again.

She ended on a wistful fade into the last soft notes.

And heard a shaken sigh behind her.

She twisted on the bench, startled yet not, because she'd conjured him, hadn't she? He was the only thing that would heal this fractured heart of hers.

He looked beautiful. He always did. Even jet-lagged, with dark circles under his eyes and that shadow coming in on his jaw, he was sexy and mesmerizing. If he'd been wearing a tie, it had since been discarded. His collar was open, his hair tousled by the wind.

"Why didn't you tell me?" he asked in a voice thickened by emotion.

"That I got into this program? I thought Nemo would. Or that it would be obvious that that's why we were here in New York." She rose and nervously gathered her sheet music into its folder, using the moment with her back to him to pull her emotions back into their compartment. Or at least try, not that it was really possible around him.

"Your mom told me you were here." He was closer.

She slid out from behind the bench and turned to face him.

He was taking her in with a gaze that ate her up from ponytail to sneakers, snagging on the sleeves of her flannel top tied around her waist, over the denim skirt and ribbed long-sleeved top.

She hugged her folder in front of her. She was only eight weeks, not showing yet, but she felt as though her belly were round and obvious.

"When did you talk to her?" she asked in a voice strained by the joy of seeing him and the panic accosting her as she tried to figure out whether she ought to tell him or—

"She invited me to lunch. She thinks you're pregnant."

"Oh." She slumped onto the keys—pretty much a capital offence—and popped off before the keys had finished resounding. Her body went hot. Her mind scattered.

The only thing she could think was, *I'm not ready for this.*

"Are you?"

"I wanted to tell you myself," she said into the folder she was still clutching.

"Then why haven't you?"

"Because you'll say we should get married."

His breath choked out as though she'd kicked him in the stomach.

"Not because..." She lifted her head and stepped forward, holding out a hand in plea. "I was planning to tell you after I've had my twelve-week scan. It's a lot less likely anything might go wrong after that so... I was trying to keep you from having to go through something painful if…" She trailed off and shrugged.

"So you would have gone through that *alone*?" He swore and ran his hand down his face. "I told you to call me if you needed anything."

"I didn't. I'm fine."

"Are you?" He raked his gaze over her again, then waved at the piano. "Because your song made me feel like my heart was being carved out with a rusty spoon."

"It's supposed to," she mumbled, not entirely displeased to hear that.

Beyond the door, laughing voices walked by.

"Let's go to my apartment so we can talk properly," he said.

She pushed her folder into her shoulder bag, but when he reached to take it, he caught her wrist and stared at the ring.

"If you don't want to marry me, why do you still wear it?"

"To keep men from hitting on me." That was true, but the least of the reasons she kept wearing it. She liked feeling connected to him.

Yes, she was still harboring those old dreams, even though he had pushed her away. She handed him the bag and pushed her hand into her pocket.

His car was outside, but they didn't talk on the short ride.

Walking into the penthouse was surreal. She'd been here for less than twenty-four hours two months ago, but it felt as though it had been years since she was here. At the same time, it was homey and familiar, as though she was returning to where she ought to be, maybe because it was stamped with his personality and everything about him felt like home.

Then she spotted the piano that hadn't been there before.

Oh, Konstantin.

"Look." She turned to face him. "I have no intention of keeping this baby from you—"

"Only yourself?" he bit out.

"That's not fair. You didn't want me," she reminded him. "And now you do because I'm pregnant? Listen to how insulting that is. I have loved you my whole life, Konstantin. I deserve to be loved back."

"You do," he agreed. "I do love you, Eloise."

"Oh, *don't*!" she cried, hurt beyond measure that he would lie to her after everything else.

"I also deserve that skepticism," he said gravely. "Refusing to say it and walking away when we could have been together all this time wasn't fair to you. It wasn't fair to us." He ran his hand over his face and took a few restless steps across the room. "It felt too good, Eloise. Hope is not something that ever worked out for me. Things would get better with my father and I would hope. He'd get a job and I'd get a gift and I would hope. My mother would pack our things and we would try to leave and I *hoped*."

She bit her lip, wanting to rush toward him, but his tension held her off. She stayed still and quiet and let him spill out what he needed to say.

"I went to live with my grandfather and there was food and peace and I thought that would be my life, but I was sent to a bloody boarding school where it was a different kind of chaos. I mastered my schoolwork and thought I'd be an architect like my friend, but my grandfather had a stroke and…" His shaken sigh spoke of untold pain. "I honestly thought I was headed back to square one at that point. That all was lost. Again. But Ilias stepped in. He made me believe there were people in this life who cared about me. That *I* could have good things. Then he *died*."

Oh, Konstantin. She swallowed his name and hurried to brush away her tears, stifling her sobs, not wanting to distress him, but he was ripping out her heart.

"And you. All you did was look at me with hope. As though I could make you happy. I don't know what happiness *is*. I've had a fleeting glimpse of it here and there, but it was always gone as quickly as it arrived. I don't know *how* to be happy. I don't trust it. I didn't trust us." He turned to face her, expression creased with remorse. "So I threw us away."

"I never meant for you to think I expect to be happy all the time. I know life is messy and painful. Look at this baby." She waved at her middle. "I'm ecstatic about it, but the best-case scenario is that it's going to hurt like hell when it arrives. I don't expect you to make me happy, Konstantin. I just want you to be with me when I am. To share it with me."

He closed his eyes, seeming to take a minute to absorb that.

"Do you really want that?" he asked solemnly. "Because I want that, too. I want to be with you even when you're not happy. I can't stand to think of you hurting and alone. I want to be there to hold you and help you and somehow find our way back to the good times because I've realized that even if those happy times only last a minute, it's a minute worth fighting for. I want those minutes, Eloise. If I miss another one, I think it might actually kill me."

"Oh, Konstantin." Her mouth wouldn't form the smile that wanted to bloom. Her lips were quivering because she was too moved. "You realize this is one of those minutes right now? That I'm really, really happy just because you're *here*?"

He swept forward and gathered her up so she was eye

to eye with him. She looped her arms behind his neck and their noses grazed and her legs were draped against his. He started to kiss her, then drew back. "Is this okay—?"

"It's perfect. I love you."

"I love you, too."

The press of his mouth against hers was so sweet it was painful. They held it to just that, a press, waiting for the agony to pass before the joy of reunion tangled with need and combusted into deprivation. In mutual attunement, they moaned and began to kiss hungrily. Passionately.

As he walked up the stairs with her in his arms, she peppered kisses against his throat.

She smiled when he set her on her feet in his massive bedroom. "Are you going to throw these away while I'm asleep?" she asked as she began to undress.

"Whatever it takes to keep you here for the rest of our lives." He paused in stripping his own clothes to throw back the covers.

Seconds later, they were under the sheets, naked bodies brushing and hands moving with familiarity over each other. She paused to trace his ear and study his rugged features, savoring this moment.

"I'll be gentle," he promised.

"I'm not worried, just letting myself feel it. This is my dream come true. I really, really love you, Konstantin. Don't break my heart again."

"I won't. I swear." His expression flexed with emotion. "I really love you, too. I'll spend the rest of my life proving it."

They kissed again and this time, the need to be reunited in the most basic way overtook them. They shifted and caressed. She opened her legs and he slid between them. His flesh prodded hers and found a warm, sleek welcome. They both sighed.

When he was deep inside her, he rolled, bringing her atop him and they lay like that a long time, kissing and caressing and simply reveling in the joy of being intimately connected.

All good things come to an end, though. And when they rolled apart a few minutes later, still panting and breathless, they smiled at each other because, really, it was only the beginning.

EPILOGUE

Five years later...

"KONSTANTIN," ELOISE WHISPERED and poked him in the side.

"Is Ilias up?" He yanked his head off his pillow and threw his leg toward the side of the bed. "I'll get him."

"No, shh. Look." She curled into him as she showed him the baby monitor where their four-year-old daughter, Rhea, was sneaking into Ilias's room. "Someone can't wait for Christmas."

"This one is for you." Rhea dropped a wrapped gift over the rail of the crib. "I got it for you."

"It's not even six," Konstantin said with wincing glance at the clock, but he shifted so he could get his arm more securely around Eloise while they watched their children.

Eighteen-month-old Ilias was sitting up, blinking with sleepy confusion in the glow of the night-light. His sister climbed onto the hamper and into the crib with him. Once she was inside, Ilias grinned and crawled toward her. They shared a little cuddle, something they did every morning, but it still made Eloise clasp a hand over her heart.

"God, they're magic," Konstantin whispered, even though the kids couldn't hear them. "They're the best thing you've ever given me. Except you, of course." He kissed her brow.

"Back at you, handsome." She curled her leg onto his strong thigh, sighing with bliss.

Aside from caesarian deliveries due to late term pre-eclampsia, both pregnancies had been uneventful, with the added bonus and delightful coincidence of their son being born on Konstantin's birthday. Konstantin didn't like to tempt fate, though. Much as he adored their children, he'd had a vasectomy and they'd agreed that if they wanted more children in the future, they would foster or adopt.

"You can open it," Rhea was saying to Ilias, pushing the present she'd brought him toward him. "Like this." She picked at the paper to start a tear, showing him.

Ilias tore little bits, making Rhea giggle.

"No, like this." She showed him how to get a longer strip.

There was some rustling and tussling and more giggling from both of them until the box was revealed.

"You did it!" She clapped her hands.

"Dit!" Ilias copied her, grinning and bouncing on his knees.

"Do you want to play with it? It's a *xylófono*."

"They already have one," Konstantin scolded good-naturedly.

"*Only* one. Rhea wants to play duets."

"Lucky us."

Eloise grinned, but their daughter's little fingers hadn't left the piano from the time she'd crawled over and pulled herself up on it. Ilias was equally fond of sitting with Mamá to help her play. Konstantin always listened with patient appreciation to any recital and encouraged both children when they showed any type of curiosity, musical or otherwise.

Ilias watched his sister, but Rhea set the box down in frustration.

"We need Bampá to open it," she said with a pout.

"Bampá." Ilias promptly stood against the rail and called out more imperiously, "Bampá!"

"Christmas morning is officially here," Konstantin said wryly, rolling to send tingling sensations down her back with the sweep of his hand as he pressed her to the long stretch of his warm frame. "I was hoping we'd start the day the way we usually do, but traditions change, hmm?"

"The good news is, we can start a tradition of napping in the afternoon. We're all going to need one."

"I like the sound of that." He brushed the tip of his nose against hers, then touched a kiss to her lips. "Merry Christmas, *angele mou*. Have I told you lately that I love you?"

"Not since last night, but—"

"Bampá!"

"But you can make it up to me later," she assured him with a chuckle.

They climbed out of bed to dress and spend Christmas with their children.

* * * * *

Were you swept off your feet by
Husband for the Holidays?

Then don't miss these other dazzling stories
by Dani Collins!

Awakened on Her Royal Wedding Night
The Baby His Secretary Carries
The Secret of Their Billion-Dollar Baby
Her Billion-Dollar Bump
Marrying the Enemy

Available now!